FINDING MISS McFARLAND

By Vivienne Lorret

FINDING MISS McFARLAND

The Wallflower Wedding Series

VIVIENNE LORRET

AVONIMPULSE
An Imprint of HarperCollinsPublishers

Excerpt from *Daring Miss Danvers* copyright © 2014 by Vivienne Lorret.

Excerpt from *Winning Miss Wakefield* copyright © 2014 by Vivienne Lorret.

Excerpt from *Full Exposure* copyright © 2014 by Sara Jane Stone.

Excerpt from *Personal Target* copyright © 2014 by Kay Thomas.

Excerpt from *Sinful Rewards 1* copyright © 2014 by Cynthia Sax.

EPub Edition AUGUST 2014 ISBN: 9780062315786

Print Edition ISBN: 9780062315793

AM 10 9 8 7 6 5 4 3 2 1

For my sisters and all the stories we share

Delaney McFarland raced to her bedchamber. The soles of her half boots slid on the carpet as she reached for the bell pull. Her father was going to kill her, dire errand or not.

"Late for your own debut?" her sister asked from the doorway, as if it weren't completely obvious. Yet even laced with censure and false surprise, Bree's voice managed to sound lyrical, adding to her list of *innumerable* charms. "Father will not be pleased."

"You think so? All this time I thought he enjoyed being ridiculed by his peers." Delaney yanked off her walking gloves with such force that she nearly toppled a pair of figurines on her side table. She reached out to secure them.

Just then, the dour-faced Miss Pursglove emerged from the hall like a wraith bent on reaping indecorum instead of souls. Then again, perhaps souls as well. "As I mentioned *before* you went out"—her austere gaze dipped pointedly to the table—"haste will only lead to further disaster, Miss McFarland."

Delaney's grip on the dainty porcelain lamb tightened. Squaring her shoulders, she faced her wretched decorum instructor. The impulse to hurl the figurine at the woman's head was so potent she could taste it. However, since she didn't have time to deal with the inevitable shards and resulting shrieks, she carefully set it back down.

"That is where you have it wrong, Miss Pursglove. Haste aids those who possess the resolve to accomplish many tasks at once," Delaney said as she deftly unbuttoned her spencer and shrugged out of it. "Whereas I find that those who waste time lurking in doorways with their lips pursed in disapproval rarely accomplish anything of merit with their lives."

Seeing those dark eyes narrow in indignation, Delaney felt triumphant. Unfortunately, the feeling was all too fleeting. For in the next moment, when she tugged off her hat and tossed it onto the bed, her sister's gasp filled the chamber.

"Your hair!" Bree's hands flew to her mouth and then to her own golden tresses, as if to make sure they were still in order. And of course, they were. Nothing was ever out of place on her sister. Her golden locks were perfectly coiffed without a strand out of place, her creamy complexion unmarked by freckles, her eyes an acceptable shade of China blue. "It looks like...like a flaming owl's nest."

Automatically, Delaney's gaze shifted to the mirror above her vanity table. In the gilded oval, she saw what the damp weather and all her rushing around had done to her mane of curly, bright auburn hair. She fought back a shudder, not wanting to reveal how much the sight shocked even her.

"Tut-tut, Miss Bree. A true lady must censor her thoughts. Do not allow a bad example to taint your own actions. A purse

of the lips is usually enough to show disapproval or even…
pity." Miss Pursglove sniffed and turned to leave. "Now, it is
time to allow your sister to apply her resolve to the *monumen-
tal* task before her."

Without another word, Bree followed Miss Pursglove out
of the room. In the same moment, the maid rushed in and let
out an *eek* of surprise before she managed to collect herself.

Delaney sagged onto the stool and stared at the assort-
ment of brushes and combs on the vanity and then back at
her reflection. "Pull the bell once more, Tillie. We're going to
need reinforcements."

Three maids, four brushes, and one olive-oil-and-lavender
hair tonic later, Delaney stood at the top of the stairs.

"Where in the blazes is she?"

She fought the urge to roll her eyes at the sound of her
father's bellow. It wasn't her fault that she'd had an emergency
errand to run or that her hair refused to cooperate. Again.

"I'm here, Father," she said as she descended slowly, hoping to make a grand entrance. If nothing else came of her
debut this evening, her impeccable sense of style would surely
be buzzing on everyone's lips.

Trimmed in silver thread, her white gown was an airy
confection with a rounded train that trailed a single step
behind her—*two steps would have been ostentatious, after all.*
The silk draped perfectly to conceal the generous curve of her
hips. An extra flounce added to her bodice gave the appearance that she did, in fact, have a bosom. Or very nearly did.
Her sleeves puffed just enough to accentuate the line of her

shoulders and throat, where the sun hadn't caused a single freckle. And at her neck, she wore the amethyst pendant her mother had given her, knowing it would draw attention to her eyes, which she'd been told were her best feature.

Gil McFarland turned away from the maid Delaney had sent ahead of her and spared a glance up the staircase. *Only a glance.* Beneath wiry auburn brows, his wintry blue gaze barely acknowledged his daughter. In fact, if it hadn't been for the quick frown amidst his hard-set features, she wouldn't have known he'd seen her at all. Clearing his throat, he looked down to the open watch in his hand before closing it with a succinct click.

The maid jumped at the sound and quickly scurried through a side door.

Yes, Delaney admitted to herself, *I'm late. I'm always late. Therefore, it should be no surprise. In the very least, he should expect it by now.* It seemed that the harder she tried to be on time, the tardier she became.

"You look rather dashing, Father," she said, hoping to earn another glance and perhaps a similar compliment. Regardless, it was true. For a man nearing a half-century old, he wore his blue coat remarkably well. In addition, his snowy white cravat complemented the silver streaks in his hair and gave his usually ruddy complexion a healthy glow. Of course, that could have more to do with his rising temper than the cravat.

"Even at your own debut, you manage to be the last to arrive," he growled, proffering his elbow. When she didn't instantly slip her hand atop his forearm, he snapped his fingers with impatience. "The most eligible gentlemen will all be spoken for by the time you make your entrance."

She blew out a breath, trying not to let her disappointment turn into irritation and then from there into anger. Like
her father, her temper was quick to ignite.

"If that is true, then they could hardly be eligible in
the first place. Either that, or they are recklessly impulsive
and would not do for *your* son-in-law," she added with the
convincing smile of serenity she'd learned to perfect when
in his presence. "We both know how little you tolerate
spontaneity."

His teeth ground together, but he held his expression in
check. "There was no reason for you to rush out this afternoon, especially when you know how long it takes you to
dress."

"Haversham's sent the wrong order, Father. What was I
to do, stare at a packet of Corinthian blue thread and two
silver needles—which obviously weren't mine—while my
Belgian lace was lost forever? Clearly, you know nothing
about the importance of lace." She'd given up hope that he
ever would.

"Besides," she continued, "I made three new friends
because of the mix-up, and we've decided to form a needlework circle. We're going to meet twice a week. Also, I've
invited them all to my debut this evening as well."

"A needlework circle?" That earned her a look at least,
albeit one of speculation. "Tell me, do your new friends know
you've never spent ten minutes sitting in a chair, let alone
plying a needle for any amount of time?"

She didn't answer, and instead turned her gaze to the liveried footmen standing guard at the wide ballroom doors.
Her failures as a daughter as well as a young woman were a

constant topic between her father and Miss Pursglove—the same woman who'd recommended that Delaney hold off her debut for two years until she was more *palatable to society*.

Now, at twenty, she was hardly the age of a debutante. Yet according to her father, her sizable dowry would make any true gentleman overlook her advanced years, in addition to any of the perceived wrinkles in her character that Miss Pursglove had not managed to iron out.

Seeing herself through her father's eyes, Delaney resembled an expensive gown, adorned with jewels but two years out of fashion and horrendously crumpled.

And as such, she would remain. Because no matter how many times Miss Pursglove tried to cram her into the mold of society, Delaney remained true to herself.

Yet when the ballroom doors opened a moment later, it felt as if every one of her flaws was on display. Beneath the gleam of the chandeliers, her confidence wavered.

In the seconds she stood with her father on the landing overlooking her guests, six recalcitrant curls snaked free of their combs. It was entirely possible that she was beginning to look like Medusa. Her hips felt as if they were expanding by the second. Not only that, but she came to the conclusion that one more flounce would have made all the difference.

More than half of the faces looking her way were complete strangers. The frenzy in her stomach was an admonishment for being late. If she'd been on time, she would have met them all, one by one, as they'd arrived. Even though she rarely gave into mawkishness, she really wished her mother were here instead of tending to her sickly aunt and cousins in the colonies.

Delaney drew in a breath. In her mind's eye, she pictured a flame burning brightly inside her as a source of determination. The warmth of it spread through her veins, bolstering her confidence.

If nothing else, her father's fortune guaranteed a grand debut. That alone would earn her a few marriage proposals by the end of the Season. No matter what she might wish otherwise, she was under no delusion that her appeal was greater than her dowry. Even a premier beauty like her mother had gained a husband who'd only wanted her fortune. Delaney could not hope for more. Or *should not*, rather.

The next hour was a blur of introductions. All in all, she received verbal invitations to eight dinners, five balls, three opera performances, and a standing invitation for walks in the park—the last of which came from her trio of new friends.

Of all the invitations, the final one from Penelope, Emma, and Merribeth had felt the most sincere to Delaney. They greeted her with genuine smiles and even laughed at how they'd met mere hours ago. And what were the chances that they would all happen to live on Danbury Lane and share an interest in needlework?

Well…at least the three of *them* shared an interest in needlework. However, since friends had not always been easy to come by—and keep—Delaney vowed to put every ounce of effort she possessed into *finding* an interest in needlework.

Too soon, her father moved her away from her new friends. It was time to greet her mother's cousin and her eldest daughter, who'd had her own debut a week ago. Neither Edwina nor Elena Mallory possessed the bright golden beauty of Delaney's mother's side of the family. They were dark featured with narrow noses that appeared pinched, as if they'd caught a whiff of spoiled milk. Of course, Delaney knew she was being uncharitable, but the truth was, her cousins had earned her censure over the years. She didn't dare let down her guard with these two.

Elena stepped forward and looped her arm through Delaney's. "Come," she said as she urged Delaney to one of the settees lining the outer rim of the ballroom. "I will give you the perfect excuse to rest for a moment."

But Delaney didn't need to rest. In fact, she always had too much energy to expend. "I really should stay with my father until we've greeted all the guests."

"Nonsense. We'll only take a moment." Elena reached toward a mahogany wine table for a crystal cup of pale lemon punch with a single raspberry floating on top. "Here. You must be thirsty after so many introductions."

"Thank you." She *was* thirsty. Between the chandeliers and the dozens of bodies in a single space, the room was rather warm. She took a grateful swallow, draining nearly half the cup. Then she puckered. This punch was far too sour. The tartness lingered unpleasantly on the back of her tongue.

Her cousin leaned forward and took the cup, placing it onto the table for her. "I imagine it's especially difficult for you."

Delaney heard the sly inflection in her tone but tried to pretend otherwise. "Oh?"

"With so much of society here because of your father's fortune," Elena clarified, as if not wanting to veil the insult.

"Then again, that is the way of things with your side of the family. All the men marry for money. It would be impossible for you to tell a genuine friend from an enemy or if a man were interested in you or in your *dowry*. But I'm sure you've already fretted over it, since you've had those additional years before your debut."

"How kind of you to point that out, cousin." Delaney tried to smile but found that the sourness on the back of her tongue had traveled downward and seized her stomach in a terrible grip. It was like the time her mother had made her wear a corset.

It took her a moment to realize it wasn't a flare of temper that was making her feel this way. Obviously, the nervous frenzy in her stomach didn't agree with the tart punch.

"Of course," Elena said, all sincerity. "I couldn't sleep at night if I didn't offer a kindly meant warning. You should know what to expect. I hate to say this, but there are true wasps amongst the *ton*. They'd just as soon smile at you as sting you in the back."

Another terrible grip seized Delaney's stomach. Damp perspiration caused a wave of heat over her scalp and down her nape. She looked to the doors, frantic for a waft of cool air, but they were closed.

Rising unsteadily, she gripped the back of a nearby chair. "Your candor is much appreciated."

"Cousin, are you unwell? With your unfortunate coloring, it's so difficult to tell." Elena rose from the settee, her head tilted to the side, more in observation than concern. "Truly, you look quite ill."

"Ill?" her father said, clearly displeased, as he joined them. "What's this about?"

"It must be nerves," Edwina Mallory offered, sidling up beside her daughter. "Every debutante has them, no matter her age."

Her father's frown deepened. "You've picked a damnable time to suffer your first case of nerves."

"I believe it was the—" *punch*...she almost said, but at the mere thought of the sour concoction, her stomach seized again. "I need air."

Delaney must have looked truly alarming, because her father ushered her toward the doors without another word. He grasped her arm just above her elbow and steered her through the crowd.

At the far side of the room, they paused as a gentleman came forth and opened the doors. "If I may be of assistance, sir."

Delaney didn't bother to look at him to determine if he was one of those she'd been introduced to or not. She continued forward, out into the brisk evening air, and gripped the marble balustrade that overlooked their small garden. A shiver rushed over her as the early spring breeze collided with the fine sheen of perspiration covering her skin.

"And you are?" she heard her father ask the gentleman who'd followed them onto the terrace.

Another spasm gripped her, this one climbing up her throat.

"Griffin Croft, sir. My apologies. My father would have liked to have made the introduction, but he was unable to attend."

"Croft," Gil McFarland said, apparently oblivious to his daughter's desire for solitude. "Your father is Marlbrook's heir."

"Yes, sir," Mr. Croft replied, his tone cooling by degree. "Though to me, he's much more than a gateway to an earldom. If you'll excuse me."

Delaney had never heard anyone speak to her father in such a clipped, censorious manner. Certainly, behind his back he'd likely had his share of rivals and disapprovers, though never to his face. Gil McFarland wasn't solely a man with a great fortune but a temper as well.

Curious about the man who dared to tempt the famed McFarland wrath, she released her grip of the railing and turned in time to see Mr. Croft bow stiffly before he started to leave.

"You have not met my daughter, young man." Though her father's voice was gruff, surprisingly there was no anger behind it.

Mr. Croft hesitated but not long enough to offend, just enough to spark another flame of interest on Delaney's part. She watched as he stiffened his broad shoulders as if wrestling between honor and duty. Obviously, someone in his family had wanted him to attend the party, so he must be in need of a bride—and a wealthy one at that.

The man who believed himself more than just the son of Marlbrook's heir turned back around, his arms stiff by his side. His gaze went from her father to her, and again he bowed.

"Mr. Croft," her father said, not bothering to conceal the satisfied grin he wore. "It is my pleasure to introduce you to my eldest daughter, Gillian Delaney McFarland."

This was the first time her father had used her full name during an introduction. Normally, he preferred not to be reminded that such a creature was named after him. Yet at the moment, she didn't bother to question it. She was too distracted by the man across from her.

Griffin Croft stood an inch taller than her father, with waves of dark hair brushed back from his forehead. In this light, she couldn't tell if his hair was black or brown, or if his eyes were brown or blue; all she knew was that when their gazes met, she felt a strange crackling sensation beneath her palms. It felt the way she imagined a fire consumed bits of tinder—hot, bright, and skittering over the surface, igniting kindling with dozens of tiny flames.

And like a flame, her gaze became greedy, consuming every nuance of his face, from his elegantly sloped nose to his wide mouth, and from the deep cleft in his chin to the square jaw and the barest shadow of stubble she saw above a clumsily tied cravat.

"Miss McFarland."

She didn't hear him at first. There was an odd ringing in her ears. But by looking at his mouth—and a very pleasant one, it was—she could see that he'd spoken.

Miss McFarland...and with those words, his lips pressed together twice. Like a kiss. The idea made her dizzy.

"Mr. Croft."

A wave of heat assailed her. Then, too soon, another terrible grip seized her stomach. Her vision blurred for an instant, and when she looked down, she saw that he held out his gloved hand, as if to steady her.

Her father's hand went to her back. "Perhaps it would be best to postpone—"

He never had a chance to finish.

And she never had the chance to turn around and take hold of the railing. Instead, her body betrayed her most cruelly and cast up her accounts all over Griffin Croft's shoes.

CHAPTER ONE

One year later

Peering over the rail and down the stairs, Delaney watched Miss Pursglove disappear through the front door. If nothing else, that horrid woman was punctual about her morning errands.

The moment Hershwell, their head butler, closed the door with a click, the air seemed to lift instantly. Delaney drew in a satisfying breath, turned on her heel, and headed in the direction of the morning room.

Buckley was already at his post. Hunched over the gilded writing desk, his pale halo of curls moved in time with the feverish scratching of the quill over the page in the ledger. They'd been meeting in secret each morning for the past few weeks. Of course, it wasn't common practice to teach one's servant a trade. For that matter, it most definitely wasn't common to hire a youth with only one arm to perform the duties of a groom—or *tiger*, rather. But

Buckley wasn't like anyone else. While he was only eleven years old, he seemed to possess a streak of determination that rivaled hers.

"Your report, Mr. Simms," Delaney said as she moved behind him and looked over his figures.

"I heard Mr. Croft speaking to Lord Everhart. He said that his last horse was a real bone-setter. So I expect he'll be at Tattersalls this morning." Impertinent as ever, Buckley didn't even look up but dipped the quill into the inkpot and continued his accounting lesson. "After that, to Thomas & Bailey's for a new coat, as he'll be escorting two of his sisters to the Sumpters' musicale later this week."

Good and good. It should be easy to avoid Mr. Croft this week.

Buckley was also exceptional for his uncanny ability to blend in with his surroundings—a talent Delaney never possessed. It made him the perfect spy. She'd been employing him to keep her abreast of all of Mr. Croft's social activities since last Season. After *the incident* at her debut, she couldn't risk being seen with that particular gentleman without dredging up the past horror. Not one candidate had been tempted enough by her dowry to overlook it. Nevertheless, she'd come up with a plan.

The idea had started years ago. After constant reminders that she was little more than a living, breathing pile of money, Delaney wondered why she couldn't use her fortune to her own advantage. More than anything, she wanted to live a life of her own choosing. Regrettably, her dowry made that impossible without a husband. Her fortune would only be released once she married. Even then, freedom was not guaranteed, unless…she could find a gentleman who was willing to sign a contract, discharging half the sum to her.

The problem was that *finding* such a gentleman was not at all simple for a societal pariah. The entire matter required discretion. Therefore, in order to find herself a husband this Season, she needed to stay clear of the gossip pages. Which meant she absolutely *must* avoid Mr. Croft.

It was imperative, especially now that much more than her own financial freedom was at stake. Her plan had altered the moment she'd first met Buckley.

Surprisingly enough, she could credit her father for that. If it hadn't been for his tendency to lose his temper, she never would have discovered Warthall Place. After her father had scared off the last two maids—who'd both had brothers employed as young grooms, or *tigers*—Delaney had gone to Mrs. Hunter's agency to look into the servant registry. As it was, Mrs. Hunter had run out of candidates for tigers. And that was when she directed Delaney to Mr. Harrison at Warthall Place.

The children of Warthall Place were not born with the privileges Delaney had once taken for granted. Most were crippled and poor, abandoned by their parents and society. Mr. Harrison wanted to change their circumstances because he'd been born with a clubfoot, yet had been given the chance to prove himself. He'd spent his life in service until his benefactor died, leaving him the sole proprietor of Warthall Place. Soon after, his purpose had shifted to finding others like him and giving them a sense of purpose. In a way, he'd given Delaney a sense of purpose as well.

"Watch that you don't mistake those nines for fours," Delaney said, pointing to the middle of the page where Buckley had done just that.

He cursed under his breath but immediately started a fresh column.

"Language, Mr. Simms," she said with a tsk. Yet even as her words came out, a shudder coursed through her. *Blast it all!* She sounded like Miss Pursglove.

Buckley's head jerked up. He scanned the room and then looked at her. "You gave me a right proper fright. I thought *ol' Miss Gloom and Doom* was here."

Delaney fought the urge to smile. "Mr. Harrison would not like to know that one of his charges forgot his manners, would he?"

His shoulders slumped, the empty sleeve of his livery coat drooping. "No, miss."

She reached out and ruffled his curls, directing his attention back to the ledger. Apparently, her heart had a weakness for impertinent towheaded boys. "Since Mr. Croft will be absent from the park this morning, I'm going for a walk. Finish that column and then leave the ledger in my room before Miss Pursglove returns."

Griffin Croft carefully avoided the squeaky bottom stair that usually gave him away. Stepping onto the foyer rug, he headed for the door, pausing only to take his top hat.

"Ah, Griffin. There you are," his mother said, unexpectedly appearing in the doorway of his father's study. The woman had ears like a bat. Likely, the whisper of beaver pelt across the glossed rosewood had alerted her to his location. "I sent your sisters to find you, but I see you managed to evade them once again."

While their home on upper Brook Street was large by townhouse standards, it still did not offer him the tiniest space for a moment of solitude. Of course, he could easily move to his own home, but the truth of the matter was...they needed him.

Slyly, he tucked his hat behind his back and returned it to the round table. "I must not have heard them."

Octavia Croft wasn't fooled for an instant. Those dark eyes of hers bored directly through his pretense. Beneath the hem of the blue morning dress draped over her plump figure, the toe of her slipper tapped against the floor. "As you know, I'm making the final adjustments to the guest list for the twins' debut."

He swallowed. This was precisely the reason he'd wanted to escape. She wanted to know if there was anyone special that he'd like to invite.

There wasn't.

More than anything, he wanted to give his mother a name, if only to ease her constant worry. Father's health was failing. After his last heart seizure, it had become harder for him to catch his breath. The title, lands, and responsibility that went with becoming the Earl of Marlbrook were closer than Griffin would have liked. The importance of his finding a bride, producing an heir, and securing the futures of his four younger sisters was foremost on everyone's mind.

His mother seemed to read the answer in his expression and let out a sigh. Retreating into the study, she smoothed the variegated brown and gray strands of hair toward the heavy bun at her nape.

"I was thinking that perhaps a walk in the park would inspire me," he said, following her.

His father was there in the study, sitting by the fire with a wool blanket over his lap. The leather upholstered wing-back chair had always been a focal point of this room, looking much like a throne and his father a king. Yet now, his father—who'd always been larger than life—had grown thin, his cheeks pale and drawn. The silk morning jacket hung over his shoulders, and the collar of his shirt gaped, exposing paper-thin flesh and the blue veins beneath.

"Good morning, sir," Griffin said, glad to see him out of the sickbed. Part of Griffin wished he were less pragmatic and dared to hope his father would make a full recovery. Unfortunately, he knew it was only a matter of time.

His father smiled with affection and lifted his reedy hand for Griffin to take. "I agree. A walk might be just the thing," his father said, giving him an encouraging pat. "Besides, you'll want to find a bride who enjoys walking out of doors as much as you do."

"What about that charming Miss Culpepper? She's only two doors down, and I see her walking with her maid in tow quite often," his mother chimed in, sitting at the desk with paper and quill at the ready.

His father made a sound. "Sickly *gel*. Walks with her nurse to improve her constitution. She doesn't get further than two doors before she has to turn back around. Not likely she'll produce any sons."

Under normal circumstances, this conversation would have made Griffin color. Discussing his need to produce a male heir in the presence of both his father *and* mother was not common practice. However, in the past eighteen months, it had become such a common occurrence that he actually caught himself nodding in agreement with his father's logic.

Griffin shook his head. Clearly, he needed fresh air now more than ever. A trip to Tattersalls to find a decent horse that didn't rattle his teeth each time he rode was necessary as well.

Before he could take his leave, his mother spoke again. "What about that Miss Danvers I saw at the end of last season? She was quite healthy-looking and pretty, in an unassuming way."

"I believe she's spoken for, my dear," his father said.

"No, you must be thinking of her friend, Miss Wakefield. It's rumored that she has been engaged for quite some time…" His mother scratched Miss Danvers's name onto the list.

His father scrubbed a hand over his jaw, his dark blue gaze turning thoughtful. "I'm certain of it. The way that Rathbun fellow hovers around her…well, if he hasn't proposed yet, he will very soon."

"There's always Miss Leeds," Phoebe, the elder of the twins, said as she walked into the study, as if this conversation were a family affair. Sure enough, Asteria, the match to the set, followed her.

Perhaps he should ask his great-uncle, the Earl of Marlbrook, to bring up the topic in Parliament. Griffin closed his eyes and blew out a breath. Why not? The man already saw him as a complete failure, so this shouldn't make the least bit of difference.

"Gads, no!" Asteria said, plopping down on the tufted hassock at father's feet. "Have you heard Miss Leeds laugh? I couldn't bear it, even if I had to endure her only for family dinners."

"True." Phoebe clasped her hands behind her back as she peered over their mother's shoulder at the list. "And not Miss Danvers. I'm certain she's spoken for."

Their father cleared his throat to hide a chuckle.

Their mother took offense, pointing the tip of her quill sharply to the paper. "She is *not* yet engaged."

"Yes, but have you *seen* Lord Rathburn?" Asteria sighed as she fiddled with the looped braids on either side of her head, making sure her chestnut tresses were in place. "Griffin wouldn't stand a chance."

For that, he tweaked one braid. It pulled free of the twisted configuration at her nape. She stuck out her tongue, proving to him that his sisters were far too young to be out in society.

"Your brother is five times more handsome than Lord Rathburn," his mother declared, soothing his slightly bruised ego.

Mischief glinted in Phoebe's dark eyes. "You only say that because you're his mother. Besides, he's…Griffin. No wonder he's having trouble finding a bride."

"What's that supposed to mean?"

His mother, father, and the twins exchanged a look.

"You have to admit that you're rather particular." This proclamation came from the doorway as Calliope—the eldest of his sisters—walked in, her gaze lifted up from her book just enough to keep her from stumbling over the fringed edge of the carpet. "After all, Miss Ambry was the toast of the Season last year, yet you said her eyes were too plain and her smile too brittle."

Tess, the youngest, skipped in next, her honey colored tresses held in place by a crown made of blooming purple chives and yellow daffodils. "You only danced with her once. Mother told me."

Oh, good. Now everyone is here at last. No need for Parliament after all.

"Then there was Miss Langfeld," Calliope added as she turned the page and settled into the window seat. A lock of dark golden hair fell unnoticed across her forehead. "I believe you said she was too quiet and prone to blushing."

Exasperated, Griffin looked to his father, only to see him grinning from ear to ear, his shoulders vibrating with barely concealed laughter. *Et tu, Father?*

George Croft coughed and attempted a stern expression. "A man knows when a man knows. Now, we just need to give Griff some space in order to find the one who suits him best."

"Oooh! Phoebe and I have that all figured out," Asteria announced, jumping up from the hassock.

When all eyes turned to Phoebe, she grinned in a way that filled Griffin with dread. The twins were too mischievous by half. How could his parents think to unleash them on society? They were only eighteen. Besides that, Calliope was not yet married…although she'd decided long before she'd reached three and twenty that she would never marry. Not after what had happened in Bath, at any rate.

In addition, it didn't help matters that his mother was bound and determined to plan a wedding by year's end. Especially now that the daughter of her younger sister would be married soon. At least one of Octavia Croft's own children was getting married—she'd make sure of it.

"Since we are about to grace society with our presence," Phoebe began, grinning like a devil, "we thought it only right to know beforehand how to decide which man we want to have pursuing us."

"Or rather, which *two* men," Asteria corrected, looking rather impish herself.

"I believe you have it the other way around, girls," their father corrected, regal wisdom in his tone. "The *man* is the one who decides which woman will make the best wife for him."

The women in the room exchanged sly smiles. Curious, Griffin sought Calliope's gaze for confirmation. She tilted her head in something of a shrug, as if refusing to be the one to shatter their father's illusions, and went back to her book.

He shook his head, more inclined to his father's way of thinking than that of the Croft women. After all, it was the man's responsibility to protect and guide the fairer sex. However, he was a gracious enough brother not to point out their patently flawed notions.

"And how would you have asked me to dance that first time, if I hadn't dropped my fan at your feet, hmm?" Octavia asked, lifting her brows at her husband. "Then I had my mother invite you to dinner. It was only later, when I took you on a tour of the gallery, that you were finally bold enough to hold my hand."

His father blinked. "If I remember correctly, you said your hand was cold."

"Did I?" She beamed. "I don't recall."

"Saucy minx," George murmured with affection.

Phoebe cleared her throat. "Clearly, a young woman sends a gentleman signals, indicating her interest. Dropping a fan at his feet and adding his name to the invitation list are more obvious examples."

"But we could just as easily flatter a gentleman's appearance," Asteria added. "Or send a compliment of his character by way of his sister."

"Then, perhaps remark on his mother's fine sense of style in order to gain an invitation to an intimate family dinner."

Calliope looked up from her book. "She will also dissuade his pursuit of any other woman, but in a way that does not make her own character appear lacking."

"She might even put herself in the path of danger, simply to have you come to her rescue," Tess added with a dreamy sigh, which earned her a frown from their mother. Thankfully, this one was only thirteen and had plenty of time to lose those fanciful notions.

"All right, girls," their father said. "I think your brother has heard enough advice for one morning. I know *I* have. More and more, I'm beginning to wonder if I know my own mind or if I was just a lamb to the slaughter all these nine and twenty years."

Octavia Croft pressed her lips together to hide her smile. "Listen to your father, dears. Now, your brother is going on a walk through the park. I imagine he won't wait above ten minutes for any of you to join him."

When his mother's gaze met his, he instantly saw where the twins received their penchant for mischief. He exhaled a short sound of impatience through his nostrils but nodded his acquiescence. "Eight minutes," he announced and watched as all four of his sisters leapt from their places, rushed through the study door, and clambered up the stairs to make ready.

So much for his idea of clearing his head during a pleasant, quiet walk. Tattersalls would have to wait as well. At least at this hour, his sisters were the only terrors he was likely to encounter.

The instant Delaney saw Griffin Croft turn onto the path ahead of her, she stopped cold.

Buckley, she scolded silently, *you assured me he would be at Tattersalls!*

She wasn't prepared to see Mr. Croft so soon. This was her first glimpse of him in months, since last Season. Not that she gave him much thought.

"Why have you stopped?" Bree asked with an exasperated huff. Even frowning did not detract from her ever-annoying beauty. "If you'll recall, this walk was your idea, not mine."

"I think we've gone far enough for today."

Fortunately, Bree had turned just enough not to notice the gentleman approaching, along with those who were most likely his sisters. Equally as fortunate, the man himself had his head turned in conversation and therefore had not seen Delaney. At least, not yet.

She hadn't a moment to lose.

Bree huffed again, as if it took every ounce of strength simply to stand upright. "I'd much rather return home and perhaps drop by the sweet shop for a peppermint stick."

"You'd waste your pin money on sweets?" Delaney always looked for a way to turn her money into something of value. Of purpose. When it came to store credit, however, she had no trouble spending her father's money. Because, when she spent enough of it, he would call her into his study, demanding to know what items she'd bought. This was the only time he listened to her. The only time she had the chance to discuss the importance of a proper wardrobe. And if the argument didn't escalate to window-shattering proportions, she might even have the opportunity to talk to him about the children of Warthall Place and Mr. Harrison's mission. She hoped her tenacity would wear him down eventually. After all, she *had* convinced him to hire Buckley.

"Not *my* money," Bree answered with a smirk. "I was hoping you'd waste yours, since your allowance is far greater."

"Fine," she agreed, but only because they *must* hurry. Delaney most definitely could *not* be seen with Mr. Croft.

Prepared to head back the way they'd come, they turned on the path. Yet in the same instant, a sudden gust of wind whipped around the tree line. Delaney's bonnet went flying. With a startled exclamation, she reached for it but was too late. Caught by another gust, it rolled away. Ribbons flailing, it continued down the path like a spinning top on a slanted table.

"Your hat!" Bree began to turn, but Delaney grabbed her arm.

"No. Leave it. I...I'll get a new one. We'll stop by the milliner's on the way. And I saw a lovely shade of cerise ribbon at Haversham's the other day. Perhaps..." Her maniacal ramblings were to no avail.

Bree turned on the path anyway. "Oh, look it's Mr...." Awareness dawned on a gasp. "*Oh, dear.*"

"Precisely," Delaney whispered. Now, it was no use. They'd been spotted. First, her bonnet had betrayed her, and then her sister. She expected it of the latter, but not so much the former. It was a heavy blow.

"Miss Pursglove is forever warning you about tying your ribbons," Bree admonished.

Delaney gritted her teeth. "Which is precisely why I never do."

Appalled, she watched her bonnet finally stop directly—*of all places*—at Mr. Croft's feet. She looked up to the heavens and prayed for a sudden deluge or something that would make fleeing the scene a necessity. Unfortunately, the sky was uncommonly clear and bright. *More's the pity.*

At least when he stood erect, she was rewarded with *his* look of utter dread upon seeing the owner of the bonnet, now in his grasp.

Oh, yes. Hullo. You might not remember me, but I'm the young woman who cast up her accounts and her dignity all over your shoes on the night we met.

And just like that night, all she could do was stand there and gape in horror.

"It's like the story of Mother's fan," she heard one of the girls say as they approached.

Whatever it meant, the alarm in Mr. Croft's expression took on a new dimension. His steps slowed as if he were approaching the gallows. She, on the other hand, would rather hurry him along. *Best to get this over with sooner rather than later.*

She took a step and then two, her chest feeling suddenly tight, her heart close to bursting under the pressure. "Thank you, Mr. Croft," she said when they were at a close enough distance for conversation. "You didn't have to go out of your way for *my* bonnet." *Anyone else's but mine.*

"Oh, but he did," the youngest of his sisters said, answering for him. "Mother named us all with purpose. Griffin is a guardian and protector. I'm certain that applies to stray bonnets."

Caught off guard by the exuberance of the girl wearing a crown of flower blossoms, Delaney smiled. "Is that so?"

The girl stepped forward, a gleam of familial pride in her eyes as she gestured to each of her sisters. "The one holding the book is the oldest of us girls. Mother says her first cry was so beautiful that she named her Calliope."

Mr. Croft cleared his throat and settled a hand on the girl's shoulder. "Miss McFarland, you must forgive my manners. Please allow me to introduce my sisters."

"There is nothing to forgive," she cut in the instant she saw his youngest sister's smile fade. Delaney had a soft spot for children who didn't always follow the strict rules of society. "This amiable girl was doing a splendid job. She's quite the skilled orator."

The youngest beamed and lifted her face to her brother. Delaney didn't catch his gaze before he bent his head forward in a slight bow of concession, yet she distinctly noted the way one corner of his mouth drew tight in something of a smirk. "Then, by all means…" he said.

His sister gestured to the other two. Except for the color of their eyes, they would have been identical. "Then, because Phoebe," she said as she gestured to the one with the brown, "and Asteria," she said, gesturing to the one with the blue, "turned her into a giantess, Mother named them after Titans."

Phoebe and Asteria wore a similar expression of exasperation that told Delaney they were likely the same age as Bree, but affection for their sister was there as well.

Delaney smiled at them and then glanced to Mr. Croft in a moment of commiseration. He certainly had his hands full. When their eyes met, however, she felt a terrible constriction of her lungs.

Abruptly, Delaney returned her gaze to the youngest. "And what about your name?"

"Because I was born in autumn with the harvest, she named me Tess." She shrugged, apparently unimpressed with her own story.

"I think Tess is a beautiful name," Delaney said and went on to explain that Bree's name meant *exalted one*, and made a face for amusement's sake. "I was named after both my parents, but I go by my middle name, which is my mother's maiden name. Nothing at all interesting, like your family names."

Tess brightened again. "Do you know what it means?"

"I do," Bree said, only too eager to interject. "Delaney means *challenging*."

That earned a giggle or two. Delaney didn't mind. Talking to Mr. Croft's sisters kept her mind off of the fact that she was standing in close proximity to *him*, knowing he must be remembering the last time. How could he not? Another mark in his sisters' favor was the fact that not a single one of them backed away as if they thought she might spontaneously combust, the way most of the *ton* did, aside from her closest friends.

Mr. Croft stepped forward and held out her bonnet. His look of horror had altered to one of mild amusement and perhaps a touch of surprise. Like her, he probably hadn't expected their second official meeting to be less of a disaster than the first. "Your hat, Miss McFarland."

Her gloved hand closed over the brim, and suddenly she felt that odd crackling sensation again. She hadn't felt it in nearly a year. She'd even convinced herself that she'd imagined it. Yet here it was again, these hot little pinpricks of sensation skittering beneath the surface of her skin.

She still couldn't tell if his eyes were brown or blue, as they were shaded beneath the brim of his John Bull. Yet, quite strangely, she felt desperate to know.

"You have my eternal gratitude, Mr. Croft," she said, meaning it as a lark. Instead, the words came out breathless because her mouth and throat had gone suddenly dry. She licked her lips and then felt the crackling burn hotter as his gaze caught the insignificant action. Although for reasons she couldn't fathom, it seemed significant now.

He released her bonnet and took a step back, his brow furrowed. "A moment's gratitude is more acceptable for such an easy task," he corrected.

Of all the arrogance, Delaney's inner voice growled, sparking a flame of a different sort. Regardless, she was determined to end this encounter better than the last. She pasted on a smile. "Perhaps. Though someone less skilled in bonnet rescue might not have returned it unmangled."

A slow grin lifted one corner of Mr. Croft's mouth, as if he found her amusing. Her eyes narrowed.

Then, one of the twins nudged him, drawing his attention. It drew Delaney's, as well—but only because she needed the distraction. A look passed between brother and sister as if something important had just happened. Delaney couldn't begin to guess what it was.

That same mystery gleamed in Phoebe's brown eyes. "Our debut party is in three days. Do you think Mother could add Bree to the invitation list?"

"And, of course, Miss McFarland should attend as well," Asteria added, her grin spreading by the moment.

No. Absolutely not. Attending a gathering at the Crofts' home would only resurrect last year's incident—which would surely hinder her chances of finding a husband.

Delaney had a plan in place for her future. She couldn't risk drawing too much attention, or it would fall apart. For now, she had to do everything she could to avoid Mr. Croft and further disaster. And that included keeping Bree from entangling both of them with the Crofts.

"Actually," Delaney began, prepared to make a polite refusal. "I'm afraid—"

"Oh yes, that would be splendid," Bree answered before Delaney or Mr. Croft or anyone with any sense could stop her.

CHAPTER TWO

The following morning, Delaney waited anxiously for Hershwell to bring the *Post* into the breakfast room. She had to know if the luckless meeting with Mr. Croft in the park was on everyone's lips.

As she paced the floor, the tantalizing aroma of freshly baked buns drew her to the buffet. They looked delicious, all golden and glazed with icing. Her stomach growled, but she didn't dare eat a thing until she knew—

"Miss Danvers and Lord Rathburn are engaged!" Bree announced, rushing in and flapping the paper at her. "And you never said a word."

"Engaged?" Delaney blinked, nonplussed. Emma hadn't said anything about being engaged earlier that week at their needlework circle.

Bree drew in a quick breath and grinned from ear to ear. "*You* didn't know."

Delaney wanted to deny it—oh, how she wanted to—but instead, she kept quiet and reached for the paper.

The devil's spawn—or Bree McFarland, to the rest of the world—quickly hid the *Post* behind her back. "It serves you right. After all, you never said a word about Penelope Weatherstone's condition. I had to find out from our cousin, Elena, and she was only too happy to gloat over me."

"Since you are not part of our coterie"—Delaney stepped toward her and wondered if she could get away with paddling her sister with the serving spoon—"I had little reason to tell you of the upcoming birth of their child."

"Miss McFarland!" Miss Pursglove admonished from the doorway. "It is unseemly to speak of such things at breakfast or any other time." Her sharp gaze closed in on the hand hovering over the silver service on the buffet.

Begrudgingly, Delaney lowered her hand. "Are young women meant to pretend that their parents found them in baskets on the doorstep? Surely I am allowed to speak of such matters to my sister, who is old enough to be out in society."

"Your mother has that right, but *you* do not."

Delaney did her best to hold her temper in check and offered a stiff nod. She'd made a promise to her mother, after all.

It had been more than a year ago since Mother had come into her room to say good-bye.

"Take care of your sister while I'm away," her mother said *after a short embrace. She withdrew a handkerchief from her sleeve and dabbed the tears from the corners of her eyes. All the while, Bree's sobs echoed down the hall. "She's too much like me, I fear, and prone to heartbreak."*

Somehow, Delaney had managed to conceal her own sadness and disappointment. She'd already known that her mother wouldn't return before her debut. The arguments she'd overheard between her parents had been her first clue.

"You are stronger than she is," her mother continued, reaching out to brush the backs of her fingers across Delaney's cheek. "The way you handle yourself around your father and that horrid woman he hired makes me see how much you've grown these past few years. You, my dear girl, are ready to make a match, because I know you are too clear-sighted to fall prey to my weakness of the heart."

In other words, Delaney knew better than to believe a man would want her for any reason aside from her fortune.

Stark reality drew her out of the memory. Unlike her mother, Delaney was determined to set the course for her own life.

Now, with Bree distracted and likely wondering if her lapse in decorum would earn a reprimand, the paper went slack in her hand. Delaney snatched it, unconcerned by the reproachful *tsk* from Miss Pursglove.

Immediately, she sought the society column. As her gaze skimmed over the latest news, she let out a sigh of relief. No mention of *Mr. C*—or *Miss M*—in the park. The way Emma and Rathburn's engagement announcement appeared, it was no wonder. It looked, for all the world, as if the Dowager Duchess of Heathcoat had designed the match herself. If ever there was news, *this* was it.

She cast a longing glance at the iced buns and sighed. First things first; she must assemble her friends to uncover the mystery of Emma's sudden betrothal.

And straightaway after that, she absolutely must decline the Crofts' invitation. It was a matter of dire importance. Her future was at stake.

Griffin caught a whiff of gingerbread and smiled. Their cook, Mrs. Shortingham, knew it was his favorite. Glad that she'd remembered his birthday, he descended the servants' stairs to the kitchen. By the time he arrived, however, one of the sculleries told him that the very last of the gingerbread had been sent to his mother's parlor.

The last of it sent to the parlor on his birthday? He didn't believe it for an instant. It must be a ruse. No doubt, his sisters and mother were preparing to jump out at him shouting a boisterous "Happy birthday!"

Normally, he detested surprises, but as long as gingerbread awaited him, he could endure anything.

Wasting no time, he went to the parlor. But when he opened the door, he found another surprise altogether. Miss McFarland stood on the edge of the carpet.

Something inside him jumped.

Even though her back was to him, there was no mistaking that auburn hair. While her attire was likely the first star of fashion and perfectly in order, her hair was a different matter altogether. As it had been when their paths had crossed in the park, she wore it tied into a chaotic sort of queue that went midway down her back. The ends of a fat periwinkle ribbon knotted with the curls. Absently, he wondered if she would brush out the tangles as soon as she returned home or if she would wait until the end of the evening when she was in bed...

The errant thought startled him. The last thing he expected to imagine was the infamous Miss McFarland in such an intimate setting. She wasn't the sort that typically incited a man's lust. A man wanted curves he could mold with his hands and a mouth he could plunder. As he'd noted yesterday, Miss McFarland possessed a rather small bosom *and* mouth. *Small* and yet...captivating.

Gradually, the strands of the conversation he'd walked in on drew his attention, providing him momentary relief.

"I can't tell you how much I appreciate meeting with you today and beg forgiveness for dropping by unannounced," the tousled Miss McFarland said, shaking his mother's hand. "I simply felt it was a matter of urgency and wanted to explain in person."

This piqued his interest. What pressing matter could have brought her here, of all places?

"Of course, dear." His mother patted her hand, not once revealing his presence in the doorway. "But as I said, I think that event has long been forgotten."

Ah. Now he understood.

"You are too kind. After coming here today to decline an invitation, I feel as if I don't deserve the warm welcome you've given me. Even though an hour has passed, it seemed mere minutes to me," Miss McFarland offered graciously. "Not to mention, I don't think I've ever been in a more cheerful parlor. The colors you've chosen are so inviting that I find it difficult to take my leave."

"With such praise, I might have to insist you stay until supper," his mother said with a laugh.

This exchange brought to mind the list his sisters had mentioned yesterday, of all the ways a young woman invites a man's attention. Something to do with *remarking on the mother's sense of style to earn an invitation*. Then, there was also the compliment she'd given him about his skillful bonnet rescue. He stared, baffled. Did Miss McFarland have marital designs on him? No. It couldn't be true.

"Thank you again for the fine cake," Miss McFarland said. "It was the most delicious confection I've ever had. I do hope your cook will share the recipe with mine someday soon."

"I'll ask Mrs. Shortingham to send it this afternoon." His mother beamed. "It's Griffin's favorite as well."

Distracted, only now did he notice the empty platter and the dark crumbs on the six plates scattered on tables about the room. Apparently, gingerbread was a favorite of his sisters too. Was that truly was the last of it? On *his* birthday? His stomach grumbled in protest.

"Isn't that right, dear?" his mother asked, acknowledging him for the first time.

"Mr. Croft!" Miss McFarland turned so swiftly that her skirts bumped into the low table, knocking over a blue vase of daffodils. Golden flowers shot out amidst a spray of water as the vase clattered against the serving fork, sending it on a path toward a bowl of frothy whipped cream. The bowl turned end over end, splattering cream along the way until it finally ended up facedown on the carpet.

"*Blast*," she cursed under her breath.

For reasons beyond his understanding, he took unaccountable delight in startling Miss McFarland. Stranger still, he found himself beguiled and intrigued by her. As he knew from the moment they'd met, Delaney McFarland was a catastrophe waiting to happen. Why this pleased him today, when it certainly hadn't before, he had no idea.

He sprang into action and rounded the table just as Miss McFarland bent down. She was frantically putting the flowers back into the vase and even trying to capture the water as the apologies tumbled from her lips.

"Mrs. Croft, I'm so sorry. How dreadful. After such a lovely hour—"

"Don't worry about it, dear. These things happen." His mother bent to rub a hand over Delaney's shoulder before she moved to the door. However, he knew that if any of his sisters had said *blast* within his mother's hearing—which was any room in the house—she wouldn't look nearly so cheerful. "I'll see if I can find a damp cloth for the cream."

Griffin stared after his mother's retreating figure, curious as to why she wouldn't simply summon a maid as she'd done for the entirety of his life, especially since mishaps like this happened every day.

When he lifted the bowl and saw a mound of cream on the carpet, he was at a loss for what to do. The best thing, he supposed, was to put the cream back into the bowl. He scooped up as much as he could with his hand, but it began to liquefy almost instantly.

"Your hands must be too warm," Miss McFarland said at the same time the thought occurred to him. "Perhaps the serving fork..."

They reached for it at the same time, his hand on the tines and hers on the hilt. Their gazes collided, and the shock of it tore through him like a bolt of lightning striking the ground at his feet. He was suddenly quite aware of the hole left behind.

He'd always thought Miss McFarland's eyes were a darker shade of blue, but he'd been wrong. They were violet, dark and lush like the petals of the same flower. And her hair wasn't what he'd supposed either. He thought it merely auburn, but now he saw that the wildly curling tendrils varied from a pale gold flame, to bright sunburst, to robust red, and then to dark, rich brown.

"Your eyes are blue *and* brown, swirled together like… lake water," she said, before her eyes widened with shock, as if only now realizing she'd spoken aloud. Abruptly, she released the fork and returned to arranging the flowers. He missed the contact immediately. "I thought they were either one or the other. I couldn't tell from a distance." Her tone was matter-of-fact now, and it made him grin. Perhaps she was just as shaken as he.

"Lake water…" He couldn't let it go, not when he saw the palest pink tinge her cheeks to the same hue of her lips. "That's rather poetic. I suppose you'd compare my hair to a chestnut mane?"

She was thoroughly engrossed in her task, plucking one flower from the front of the vase and placing into the center. "More like freshly turned earth, if you must know. The color is darker toward the roots with streaks of sun bleached brown at the tips."

Another jolt tore through him at the elemental under-tone of her description. His mind conjured an image of fire cleansing freshly turned earth in preparation for planting—flames licking, like tendrils of hair caught in the wind; consuming, like eager, ravenous mouths; undulating, like bare limbs in the throes of ecstasy, while violet eyes stared up at him...

Griffin was suddenly aware of a growing arousal.

Just then, Tess bounded into the room and immediately rectified *that* situation. "Mother sent me to ask if you'd like Cook to bake another gingerbread...since it's your birthday, after all. She also wanted to know if you'd like to invite a guest for supper this evening before the musicale. Oh, hullo, Delaney."

Miss McFarland offered a smile. "It's a pleasure to see you again, Tess. That yellow frock is quite becoming on you." Then as his sister beamed and plucked at the ruffles on her skirt, Miss McFarland turned her focus on him, her violet gaze round with unease. "My errors in coming here seem to be increasing by the moment. We ate your special cake."

That she should worry he was now in want of gingerbread stirred a pleasant warmth within him. "Mrs. Shortingham will make another."

She pressed her lips together. "I made a mess of the parlor."

"Only the center," he teased but found his gaze returning to her small pink mouth, as if oddly fascinated by the shape and color. Although as far as he could tell, there was nothing particularly remarkable in either. It simply captured his attention the way a candle flame might. "The corners are still quite tidy."

"Nevertheless, I'm certain that I'm the very last person you wanted to see today," she said and straightened, smoothing down the front of her skirts. "Please accept my wishes for the merriest of birthdays."

He straightened as well, desiring to adjust the front of his cutaway and waistcoat but his hands were too sticky. "Would you like an invitation to supper this evening?"

She shook her head so abruptly that *some* men might have taken offense. "And again, my unexpected presence has put you and your family in an awkward situation. For that, I'm truly sorry and for everything else as well." She turned to Tess. "Please tell your mother that, while her invitation was most gracious, I have a previous engagement this evening."

His sister shrugged and turned, skipping down the hall to where their mother likely waited in the next room, listening to every word.

"I don't understand you, Miss McFarland," he said, studying her with new interest. "Last Season, I was nearly convinced you went out of your way to ensure that we were never seen in the same place, to avoid association to the—"

"*The incident*," she supplied quickly. "That is the only delicate way to refer to what happened at my debut, Mr. Croft."

He grinned at the haughty way she addressed him, saying *Mr. Croft* as if accusing him of a wrongdoing or misbehavior. "Then, a year after *the incident*, I cannot go three steps without running into you. Why, you practically laid your bonnet at my feet yesterday, daring me to pick it up."

Her lips parted on a gasp, offering him a flash of her pink tongue. "I did no such thing. It was the wind and nothing—I repeat, *nothing*—more."

A bit of deviltry flared to life within him. Now, he wanted to hear her haughty address again. He wanted to goad her into those three syllables. "Yet you came here to spare my mother's feelings and then stayed long enough to encourage her, praising her in a way that gave every indication of your interest in her son."

"Mr. Croft!"

He felt her admonition cover him, tightening the flesh over his bones. He could feel heat radiate from each drop of blood in his veins, feel the length of each hair on his body. His follicles contracted—released—contracted with those three syllables out of her small pink mouth.

Mis-ter Croft.

Something flashed in her gaze, like a sudden spark to gunpowder. For an instant, the violet in her irises brightened to pale lavender. She drew in a breath before she continued, her voice low and calm. "You are mistaken, sir. While I mean this as no insult, either to your person or to your family, the plans for my future in no way involve you. Good day."

Even though she was quick to leave, he knew he could catch her if he wanted to. However, he still had damnably sticky cream on his hands, in addition to a strange bruising around his ego. He had little doubt she'd meant what she said about her future not involving him. Yet he hadn't a clue why it bothered him.

On the drive home, Delaney decided that she was going to kill Bree. It was her fault, after all—at least every iota of disaster she'd experienced in these past two days. If it hadn't been for her sister, she never would have made such a fool of herself in front of Mr. Croft. Again.

Of course, she had to cast some of the blame on him too. Everything had been fine until his sudden appearance in the doorway. Then, *everything* went completely, utterly wrong. The table, the flowers, the cream, the comment about his eyes...oh, why did her mouth run so often without the intervention of her brain?

It wasn't her fault. It was his, for making her uncharacteristically nervous. She was never nervous, or prone to fits of blushing, for that matter. Yet she'd distinctly felt a surge of heat rush to her cheeks. *Blast it all!*

The conceited, arrogant, contemptible man had had more than his share of amusement at her expense too.

The only thing that had not turned into a complete catastrophe was the simple fact that the entire ordeal hadn't taken place in a public venue. Thankfully, with Emma's recent engagement to Lord Rathburn in the *Post*, the *ton* had more interesting things to talk about—at least for now.

How long could that last? Not long, she was sure.

Delaney drew in a breath. During moments like this, she became more and more focused on her plan to marry by the end of the Season. All she needed was to find a gentleman who agreed to her terms. After all, it shouldn't be too difficult to find someone who wanted her for her fortune and nothing more.

Chapter Three

The Dorset ball was a complete crush.

After Delaney's disastrous week, things were starting to look up. Naturally, to avoid another encounter with Mr. Croft, Delaney had not attended the Sumpters' musicale. Even so, tonight her spirits were high. Part of the reason, no doubt, was because she knew he wouldn't be here.

From the gallery, Delaney spied at least two possible husbands, each of them more dissolute than the other. For the first time in nearly a year, she felt her chances for marrying within her grasp.

Merribeth Wakefield joined her near the potted palms in the corner and looked over the railing as well, her face bathed in the glow from the chandeliers. "I cannot wait to see Emma dance with Lord Rathburn. They are a perfect match, though I find it odd that Emma isn't at sixes and sevens with their wedding only weeks away. I would be coming unglued, I'm certain."

"You, unglued? Hardly. You've been planning your wedding for years." Delaney playfully nudged her. "I am the one who would be forced to elope simply to keep my sanity. A blacksmith in Gretna Green is all I require. Besides, I wouldn't be able to stand still for a church ceremony."

Merribeth laughed. "Then we must find your husband amongst one of the dancers. He shouldn't be able to keep still either."

"Reginald Hargrove is one of those below," Delaney mused, staring down at the top of his balding pate. "I've learned his estate is approaching ruin after his brother bankrupted them and fled the country."

"Hargrove is nearly as old as your father." Her friend made a face that drew attention to the infamous tilt of her dark brows. "And as you said, he's nearly a pauper. Why ever would you want to marry him?"

"Who better than a man who requires a fortune when I am the possessor of one?" When her father nearly doubled her dowry after *the incident*, the indecent sum had made her a mockery. She'd even heard that the betting books at White's speculated on what it would be next year.

"Delaney, you are more than that dowry over your head," Merribeth chastised softly and squeezed her hand. "You deserve a man who sees past your fortune."

No. That would never do. Even if such a man existed, she would not marry him. She'd never risk falling in love. After seeing how the lines between money and love had ruined her own parents' marriage, she knew it was better to keep the two separate. That was the sole reason she'd come up with the plan to find a husband who needed her fortune, but one who'd gladly leave her to live her life in peace. Alone.

"Not all of us possess your steadfast romantic notions," Delaney said fondly. "Nevertheless, since Hargrove is a widower with two sons, he doesn't require an heir. That makes him practically perfect." Delaney would never have to see him past their wedding day. She could purchase a house and do whatever she wanted with her share of the fortune.

"You don't want children of your own?" Her friend looked as if she were seeing her for the first time.

"It isn't that important," she said, hating herself for the small lie. Having children would require a true marriage. Intimacy. Love. From watching her own parents, she knew that money and love could not exist together. "Besides, I'm far too cynical to be a mother."

Merribeth squeezed her hand. "I've believed for some time now that you are not as cynical as you let on."

"A true romantic *would* say that." Delaney asked, earning a smile from her friend before their gazes drifted over the ballroom. "Oh, look. I see my cousins below. Shall we beg them for a dance? I'll give you first pick, since I've no preference for Maddox over Munroe or the other way around."

"I think I'd rather watch Emma. Or rather, watch Lord Rathburn glare at her partner. Rathburn looks perfectly capable of murder." Normally, those words wouldn't be said with such delight, but they were all swept away in Emma's unexpected betrothal. "Penelope was quite right. That is a possessive look if ever I've seen one."

The moment Delaney saw it, she felt a twinge of longing. Not for Rathburn, but to have her own gentleman look at her that way. And to know that he wasn't thinking of her dowry. It was a foolish, impossible dream, she knew. One she would never reveal, not even to her closest friends.

"If I stand still a moment longer I shall explode." Delaney gripped the railing with both hands, hoping it would help her expend some of her ceaseless energy. It didn't work. "Would you forgive me for leaving you alone for one set?"

Her friend laughed. "Of course not. I'm surprised you've lasted this long."

"Give me a full report as soon as I return," she said without a backward glance as she descended the stairs, intending to dance a full set with either of her cousins.

However, when she skirted passed the potted topiary at the bottom of the stairs, she abruptly crashed into a wall. Or more precisely, a wall of Corinthian blue superfine wool and the solid gentleman beneath. She lifted her gaze...*oh*, and not just *any* gentleman either, but the ever-charming, dashing, and *penniless* Lord Lucan Montwood. Rumor had it that he was recently cut off from his family without a farthing. Quite unexpectedly, opportunity arose.

"Forgive me, I—" they both said in unison and then laughed at their syncopated mimicry.

With a rakish grin, he took a step back, snapped his arms against his sides and bowed his dark head. "Miss McFarland."

"Lord Montwood." Delaney curtsied, refusing to allow his smile or the fact that he'd remembered her name go to her head. She knew enough to realize that a young gentleman in need of a fortune must marry a young woman in possession of one. Therefore, he likely kept a list of potential candidates. If she were to fault him for knowing her name because of her dowry, then she was indeed a hypocrite. After all, they were the same creatures but in reverse.

Still, she couldn't resist the temptation to make her observation known. "I must say I'm pleased you remember my name. After all, it's been above a year since we were introduced."

His magnetic smile never faltered. "I've often wondered why we never seem to attend the same gatherings. Then again, I've also noticed that a certain…*Mr. Croft* and I frequent the same parties."

She laughed outright. It probably wasn't proper. Most likely, she should have blushed and pretended she hadn't a clue to what he was referring. But that wasn't her way. "Perhaps I keep a fervent schedule to ensure that he and I are never seen attending the same dinners and balls."

Though she said it in a teasing manner, the truth wasn't far off.

Montwood studied her closely for a moment. While his charming countenance remained steadfast, his amber eyes suddenly sharpened. "You don't strike me as the type to care whether or not the *ton* wags their tongues in your direction. So perhaps there is another reason you avoid him."

She arched a brow, wishing she had half of Merribeth's ability for censure in a single look. "That is a bold speech for someone who hasn't spoken with me above half an hour."

"Too bold?" He smiled then, flashing a dimple that was nearly impossible to resist.

"Quite."

"Then allow me to make it up to you." He glanced over his shoulder and gestured toward the dancers. "This set is nearly over, but I've no attachments for the next. That is, unless your card is full."

"I believe you already knew the answer before you asked," she said, her smile returning. "I think very few people would accuse *you* of being impulsive."

For the first time, his façade fell. In an instant, his expression turned hard and cold, revealing the rough edges of whatever it was he fought to conceal. "The few whom I consider friends understand my methods and the motivation behind them."

In that tense moment, she felt her inner flame spark. Determination filled her. The stark reality of his situation and hers collided in a flash of inspiration. Everything was about to fall into place.

"Then perhaps you would consider me a friend," she said, living up to her impulsive reputation. Yet in the next breath, she managed to shock even herself. "I have a proposition that, I believe, will aid us both in achieving our ultimate goals."

Griffin assisted Octavia Croft down from the carriage and waited in turn for Phoebe and Asteria.

"As much as I love my sister, I'm almost glad she had to cancel her dinner party this evening," his mother said, unable to conceal her grin as she stared up at the Dorset mansion ablaze with lights in every window. "Although a megrim is a terrible ordeal. I must remember to send her a box of chocolates on the morrow."

Amused, Griffin wondered if the gift would be an aid for her recovery or an expression of gratitude. "Perhaps another box of chocolates for Lady Dorset as well, for graciously receiving our party at the last minute."

"The Dorset ball," his mother breathed the words. "I remember attending these during my Seasons. Who would have thought my dear friend Hortensia would marry Lord Dorset's heir? And they have a young man just the age for my girls."

The twins linked arms on either side of their mother. "One young man for both of us, Mother?"

"That would create quite the scandal."

Octavia shushed her girls and warned them to mind their steps. If the evidence left behind from numerous horses was any indication of the number of guests in attendance, this ball was quite the crush.

"Speaking of scandal," Phoebe said with a devilish gleam in her dark gaze, "I do believe Bree McFarland and her sister will be in attendance. What do you imagine the chatter will be if you are seen together? Or perhaps even dancing?"

Griffin's shoulders stiffened as they passed liveried footmen and crossed the threshold. "As a Croft, you would do better not to mention the words *scandal* and *Miss McFarland* in the same sentence, or likely tongues will begin to waggle about *you*."

The last thing he wanted was to hear about Miss McFarland all evening. Shockingly, he'd found it difficult to put their latest encounter out of his mind.

The twins tipped forward and exchanged a look. Then, as if privy to their unspoken conversation, their mother tutted. "Girls, your brother is right. Besides, you must remember that this Season is not solely for your own benefits but for Griffin's as well."

He didn't respond. They were all counting on him to find a wife and secure the title for the sake of their family. The problem was, he wasn't any closer now than he had been a year ago. All this time, he'd wanted to feel a sense of connection with his future wife—an ability to share a single look and somehow know…everything. So far, he hadn't found that.

As they ascended the stairs, the hum of voices and swell of music flowed through the open ballroom doors, where two additional liveried footmen stood sentinel.

"I found it strange that we didn't see the elder Miss McFarland at the Sumpters' musicale the other night, especially with her father and sister in attendance," Asteria mused. When they reached the top of the stairs, their mother stepped forward to chat amicably with Lady Dorset.

Not wanting to encourage another mention of Miss McFarland, Griffin ushered the younger twin forward to be introduced to their hosts. Of course, with his sisters being of like mind, Phoebe took up where Asteria had left off.

"And I distinctly recall her mentioning she had plans for that evening, though I cannot think for what." The purposeful way her gaze slid to his told him that she was more interested in his reaction to the news and not in recounting a fact. "After all, the musicale was the only noteworthy engagement."

He'd guessed the answer already. Delaney McFarland was still avoiding him, especially after their encounter in the parlor. It seemed that whenever they were in close proximity, disaster ensued. Or perhaps it was just her way.

Again, when he ignored one sister and ushered her forth for an introduction, the other one began. "I've given this a great deal of thought, and I believe it was love sickness."

Griffin fought the urge to release an exhausted exhale to the heavens. "I'm certain you have better things to occupy your mind." He couldn't wait to find them enough dance partners to keep them too busy to meddle in his affairs.

"It's the fluttering," Asteria stated, as if she were the premier expert on love sickness.

He knew he shouldn't ask—*oh, how he knew*—because it was just like his sisters to make a nonsensical declaration and leave it at that. It was maddening. Yet they always managed to reel him in. "I beg your pardon?"

She blinked up at him as if he were a halfwit. "From love at first sight. That's when *it* happened, after all. The moment she saw you."

Phoebe joined them again. "Then you told him? Good," she said with a sigh of relief. "Now I won't have to worry about slipping up and saying it at breakfast."

"True. It's hardly breakfast conversation." Asteria shielded her eyes from the chandeliers as she looked up toward the gallery. "Oh, look. There is Bree now. I wonder where her sister could be."

Phoebe stepped forward. "Her coloring should be easy to spot. Griffin, do you see her?"

His head was spinning. If these two managed to marry, their husbands would be in Bedlam in under a fortnight. Confoundedly, he found himself scanning the room all the same.

Love sickness? The idea was preposterous...and yet somewhat diverting.

After a moment, he spotted Miss McFarland just before she disappeared around a pruned juniper in the corner and slipped behind a grand but narrow tapestry that extended from the floor to the vaulted ceiling. A prickling sensation caused the hair at his nape to lift, almost as if he sensed she was up to no good. Although he couldn't know that. He barely knew her.

"Perhaps the retiring room," Asteria said to her sister just as their mother joined them.

"Girls, I told you not to drink too much tea before we left," Octavia chastised quietly. "However, if you already need the retiring room, you'll find it up those stairs and to the right."

Griffin stared again at the tapestry that was nowhere near the retiring room and caught a glimpse of Lord Lucan Montwood disappearing behind the hidden doorway in the same moment.

The prickles at his nape turned into a full-fledged warning bell.

He knew enough about Montwood to know that a woman in possession of a fortune was not safe near him.

"I know it seems unconventional," Delaney concluded, watching skepticism darken Montwood's features.

In the scant moonlight drifting in through the conservatory windows, his brow furrowed. "You said it yourself a few moments ago—we haven't even spoken above half an hour, and here you are, offering yourself in marriage to an impoverished second son, who by all accounts will gamble away every shilling you possess."

She held up a hand to clarify. "I'm not offering myself. I'm only offering my fortune. We would keep separate addresses. You would live your life and I mine."

He shook his head. "Why would you do this?"

"If I were a man with my own means, I'd need never marry. Since I am an unmarried woman, however, I am allowed very little freedom to live how I choose. I want that freedom." She noticed her hands had clenched into fists as she spoke and made a point to relax them before she continued. "Surely I need not tell you how trying it is to require constant approval from a parent who sees every venture as a foolhardy pursuit." Rumor had it that his father was an absolute tyrant.

Now, all she had to do was convince Montwood to sign a contract that would release half of her dowry to her. When he sat down on a nearby bench and released a long exhale, it was all the encouragement she needed. Soon, she would be the possessor of her own fortune, and no one could tell her how to use it. Her inner flame flared in triumph.

She was wearing him down.

Griffin slipped behind the tapestry and entered a long arched hallway. Closed doors flanked either side. Listening carefully at the first, he heard nothing and moved on to the next. His sense of wariness grew as he neared the end of the hall. A slight jog down a narrow passage opened to a conservatory. A very dark conservatory.

The cloying scent of camellia and orange blossom greeted him as he stepped inside. Tall panes of glass formed walls that bowed out toward the garden. Yet only the barest gleam of moonlight made its way through the foliage of potted trees and hanging plants.

He spotted Miss McFarland standing near a fountain in the center of the room. Montwood was only steps away, seated on a wrought-iron bench, his expression severe and thoughtful, as if he were listening to an accounting of his sins by Saint Peter.

"I realize my proposal must seem unusual, even abrupt," she said as Griffin stepped within earshot but kept to the shadowy path between the trees. "However, I believe a marriage in name only would benefit us both. You would gain a fortune and maintain a discreet amount of freedom, while I would gain my own home, completely separate from yours."

Montwood sat forward. "And you would do this for me? For someone you hardly know?"

"Barring that you have no other obligations or romantic entanglements," she said with an ambiguous lift of her shoulders. "It is as much for me as it is for you. The sooner I marry, the sooner the betting books at White's concerning my dowry will be closed forever. And yes, I can see by the gleam in your eyes that you recognize a way to win twofold, which is fine with me."

Griffin couldn't believe his ears. A sudden rush of rage swept through him. He forcibly stopped himself from charging into the center of the room. But as he did, his sole scraped across the tile at his feet.

Miss McFarland looked over her shoulder toward the doorway and then back to her *would-be* groom. "It would be safer to speak of this if you came to call and invited me for a drive in the park."

"Tomorrow," Montwood agreed as he rose. "For now, I'll leave through the garden door and return to the ballroom by way of the terrace. That way, should you change your mind, you wouldn't be forced into marriage by threat of ruination. Good evening, Miss McFarland. You might very well be my angel of mercy."

If Montwood had so much as reached out to kiss her hand, Griffin would have charged in like a contender at Five Courts and planted a right solid facer. Thankfully, the dissolute cad slunk back into the shadows. A moment later, the faint squeak of the hinge and then the quiet click of the latch punctuated the fact that they were alone.

"Kindly reveal yourself," Miss McFarland said to the room, impatience emanating from her stiff posture. "If you'd hoped to either frighten me or begin a new rumor, I can assure you that your plans are futile. If it's money you want—"

"Has no one ever told you that money is the force that drives all evil deeds and evil-doers, Miss McFarland?"

"Mr. Croft!" She started. Her violet eyes widened as he stepped into the center of the room. Doubtless, she had no idea how those three syllables wreaked such havoc inside him. "What are you doing here?"

Gritting his teeth to control his temper and the *contract-release-contract* sensation she caused, he tugged at the square front of his waistcoat. "I might ask the same of you."

"No. I mean here, at the Dorset ball. You were supposed to be dining with your aunt this evening."

Ah. So then, his assumptions were correct. She *had* been purposely avoiding him.

He clasped his hands behind his back and began to pace around her in a circle. "Do you have spies informing you on my whereabouts at all times or only for social gatherings?"

She watched his movements for a moment, but then she pursed those pink lips and smoothed the front of her cream gown. "I do what I must to avoid being seen at the same function with you. Until recently, I imagined we shared this unspoken agreement."

"Rumormongers rarely remember innocent bystanders."

She scoffed. "How nice for you."

"Yes, and until recently, I was under the impression that I came and went of my own accord, that my decisions were mine alone. Instead, I learn that every choice I make falls beneath your scrutiny." He was more agitated than angered, not to mention intrigued and unaccountably aroused by her admission. During a Season packed full of social engagements, she must require daily reports of his activities. Which begged the question, how often did she think of him? "Shall I quiz you on how I take my tea? Or if my valet prefers to tie my cravat into a barrel knot or horse collar?"

"I do not know, nor do I care, how you take your tea, Mr. Croft," she said, and he clenched his teeth to keep from asking her to say his name once more. "However, since I am somewhat of an expert on fashion, I'd say that the elegant fall of the mail coach knot you're wearing this evening suits the structure of your face. The sapphire pin could make one imagine that your eyes are blue—"

"But you know differently."

Her cheeks went pink before she drew in a breath and settled her hand over her middle. Before he could stop the thought, he wondered if she was experiencing the *fluttering* his sister had mentioned.

"You are determined to be disagreeable. I have made my attempts at civility, but now I am quite through with you. If you'll excuse me..." She started forward to leave.

He blocked her path, unable to forget what he'd heard when he first arrived. "I cannot let you go without a dire warning for your own benefit."

"If this is in regards to what you overheard—when you were eavesdropping on a *private matter*—I won't hear it."

He doubted she would listen to him if he meant to warn her about a great hole in the earth directly in her path either, but his conscience demanded he speak the words nonetheless. "Montwood is a desperate man, and you have put yourself in his power."

Her eyes flashed. "*That* is where you are wrong. I am the one with the fortune; ergo, the one with the power."

How little she knew of men. "And what of your reputation?"

Her laugh did nothing to amuse him. "What I have left of my reputation will remain unscathed. He is not interested in my person. He only needs my fortune. In addition, as a second son, he does not require an heir; therefore, our living apart should not cause a problem with his family. And should he need *companionship*, he is free to do so elsewhere, as long as he's discreet."

"You sell yourself so easily, believing your worth is nothing more than your father's account ledger," he growled, his temper getting the better of him. He'd never lost control of it before, but for some reason, this tested his limits. If *he* could see she was more than a sum of wealth, then *she* should damn well put a higher value on herself. "If you were my sister, I'd lock you in a convent for the rest of your days."

Miss McFarland stepped forward and pressed the tip of her manicured finger in between the buttons of his waistcoat. "I am *not* your sister, Mr. Croft. And thank the heavens for that gift too. I can barely stand to be in the same room with you. You make it impossible to breathe, let alone think. Neither my lungs nor my stomach recalls how to function. Not only that, but you cause this terrible crackling sensation beneath my skin, and it feels like I'm about to catch fire." Her lips parted, and her small bosom rose and fell with each breath. "I do believe I loathe you to the very core of your being, Mr. Croft."

Somewhere between the first *Mis-ter Croft* and the last, he'd lost all sense.

Because in the very next moment, he gripped her shoulders, hauled her against him, and crushed his mouth to hers.

Chapter Four

For the first time in her life, Delaney stood perfectly still.

She didn't move. Didn't breathe. Didn't even blink her eyes.

This couldn't be happening. Griffin Croft wasn't kissing her. He wasn't lifting her to her toes in the middle of the conservatory, just steps away from the crush of the Dorset ballroom.

And yet...he *was*.

His warm, hard mouth slanted over hers. Wondrously heated breaths flared from his nostrils, igniting the air between them. Where his chin pressed into hers, she could feel the tiniest unshaven whiskers inside the deepest part of his cleft. Her breasts flattened hard against his chest, and the pounding of his heart felt like a fist threatening to break through a door. Only *she* was that door. Down the center of her back, his hand roamed. Fingers splayed, he touched every rib and vertebra as if committing her skeleton to memory. His exploration continued until that hand settled into the dip just above the rise of her derriere. And then, he drew her even closer.

If she'd worn stays, she was certain she wouldn't be able to feel the buttons of his waistcoat. Wouldn't be able to feel her nipples harden, sprouting to life beneath the layers of fine linen and silk.

The crackling that possessed her every time Griffin Croft was near burned hotter than before. Instead of pinpricks of heat, tiny flames licked over her flesh, threatening to char every inch. This time, she didn't mind in the least.

"Open for me," he growled against her lips, tilting up her chin.

It was only when she felt his other hand teasing the underside of her jaw that she realized he was no longer the one keeping her up on her toes. Well, not entirely. The hand nestled into her lower back was doing a fair job of holding her against him. Yet the arms she'd twined around his neck were doing the rest.

Impulsively curious, she did as he bade, wondering what new sensations would unfold. His staggered breath puffed against the damp underside of her lips. In that moment of hesitation, she opened her eyes, having no idea when they'd drifted closed.

What she saw in his gaze stole the last remaining breath from her lungs. It, too, came out staggered. Brown and blue colors swirled together in that beautiful lake water she'd noticed only days ago, but what she hadn't noticed was how it seemed to churn and undulate beneath the surface, as if coming to a slow simmer. The heat of it was so potent she could almost touch it with her fingertips, sure they would come back blistered.

What startled her most of all was how his gaze seemed to reflect everything inside of her.

Suddenly, she wanted to push away. "Mr. Croft, I—"

A low sound tore from his throat as he captured her mouth again. His tongue swept inside, tangling with hers, teasing her enough to follow, to taste, to traverse the ridges and valleys of teeth and palate, leaving nothing unexplored. She knew the flavor of him now. Swallowed the essence of him—the tang that was slightly salty, slightly sweet, and more pleasant than she could have ever guessed.

Wanting more of this elixir, her hands found the back of his head and drew him closer. His soft wavy hair was cool at the tips but blazing with heat at his scalp. She slanted her mouth over his in the opposite direction. This time, she nudged *his* lips apart. She sought his tongue, butting up against his in a sudden frenzy of need that sent a swift jolt of warning through her.

Something within her had awakened. Something that fed off kisses and burned with an intensity she'd never known.

Something that threatened the life she wanted for herself.

Suddenly, she broke away from him, giving his shoulders a little shove in the process. He released her instantly and stared down at his hands as if they alone were the culprits of this whole affair.

"Miss McFarland," he said, his breathing labored, his broad shoulders straining against the impeccably tailored tailcoat. "I want you to know that I had no intention of kissing you when I came in here. In fact, my thoughts were centered solely on making sure you understood the dangers of being alone with a man."

She recoiled. His words were like a slap, and one hard enough to shake the last of the fog from her mind. Only now did she realize what a fool she'd been. He'd had no intention of kissing her…as if the mere idea were abhorrent to him. For a moment, she'd actually thought he'd found her desirable—not her fortune but her person, her entire being—so much so that he couldn't help himself. And she'd responded in kind.

Hearing the truth wounded her pride more than she thought it could. "I'm ashamed to admit how well you've made your point, Mr. Croft."

He shook his head, plowing a hand through his hair. "What I meant to say was—"

"I'm sure in our limited acquaintance we've both intended for each of our encounters to unfold differently. Let's simply add this to our list of disasters, shall we?" She smoothed the front of her gown and hoped she didn't look as wrinkled as she felt. "Now, if you'll excuse me, I'd like to return to the ballroom before our names are once again joined in scandal."

As she passed, he reached out and grasped her arm. "I was speaking of Montwood. He's not to be trusted. And if his creditors see him driving in the park with you, they'll soon find a way to make him truly desperate. All I ask is that you take that under consideration."

"While I appreciate your unsolicited advice, what I do or *do not do* with Lord Montwood is none of your concern." She cast him a withering glare. "Now, if you'll unhand me, I'll bid you farewell."

He released her at once.

Delaney held her head high as she walked out of the conservatory. She only wished she didn't feel so cold inside.

CHAPTER FIVE

"Seven and twenty," George Croft said to his son, adding a whistle at the end. This morning, they sat alone in the curricle for his father's first outing in over a fortnight. "By this age, I'd been married four years and widowed one."

Griffin kept the reins steady in his grip and stared straight ahead to the park's path. This was his father's not-so-subtle way of reminding him of his duty to find a bride—and soon. "I'm attending every event my schedule will allow. Unfortunately, this year is far too much like the last." Aside from one night—the night of *the incident*—the previous Season had been tedious at best. Worse yet, the highlight of *this* Season had been a stolen moment in the Dorsets' conservatory the night before last with the same damnable woman.

"Then perhaps you aren't attending the right events. I know she's out there." His father slapped his hand across his knee. "Why, if it hadn't been for a change in my schedule, I'd never have met your mother. Three years I'd waited to remarry, waited to find the right one. The one that stood out from the rest. Then it was like a curtain parted…and there she was."

At his father's words, Griffin hoped his imagination would conjure a vision of his future bride, pointing him toward the right path. The only thing *he* saw was a peculiar swath of flame bright red obscuring his view.

It must be the sun shining against his eyelids.

"Of course, I want you to find love or at least a woman you can stand," his father added, now with a pat on Griffin's shoulder, "but a healthy woman, not like my first wife. Prudence was a pretty little thing but perhaps too young and far too delicate. Miscarried three babes before she went off to heaven to be with them, rest her soul."

Last year, Griffin had been asked to find the love of his life. This year, he was asked to find a healthy woman he could stand.

Under other circumstances, he'd laugh. However, he knew the importance of finding a bride. At fifty-seven, his father's health was fading. The only way for Griffin to give him peace of mind was to find a wife and quickly issue a male heir upon her. That way, if an accident or early demise should befall *him*, his wife, children, mother, and sisters would be well provided for and not at the mercy of a distant cousin.

He exhaled a deep breath, feeling a weight pressing against him. It wasn't as if he didn't have the desire to marry. Even before his father's cousin—his great-uncle's heir—had died of consumption, he'd thought about it. Though before that and before his father had his first heart seizure, it had seemed unlikely that Griffin would inherit. There'd been no rush. He'd simply been waiting for the curtain to part and reveal his future bride.

Now, it was a matter of great urgency, and he couldn't find one suitable woman who kindled his interest.

"What about that Miss McFarland?" his father asked, startling him. "I realize after the mishap last year that any acquaintance with her is unlikely. As I recall, it caused quite the stir. On the other hand, your mother said she was a charming girl, though not necessarily pretty."

Ignoring the sudden escalation of his pulse at the mention of that name, Griffin felt a frown pull against his brow. "Mother said she wasn't pretty?"

"She said something to the effect of a freckled complexion, hair that was too bright and wayward, and eyes a shade or two...*off.*"

"*Off,*" Griffin found himself murmuring, and he wondered if his mother had seen the same woman.

He hadn't noticed that her freckles marred her complexion. Actually, he found they added to her vibrancy, the way spices enhance a bland meal. Not only that, but to him, her hair was fascinatingly unruly. Certainly not too bright. As for her eyes, the violet was quite striking and unusual. Especially up close, with her warm breath filling his mouth, the heat of her body under his hands, and...

He shook his head to clear the memory from his mind. *Off?* Never.

Thoughts of the other night in the Dorsets' conservatory plagued him. Not only the kiss but her conversation with Montwood as well.

His hands tightened on the reins as he fought a swift rise of annoyance. "Regardless of what Mother may think of her charms, Miss McFarland is too maddening a creature for consideration. She's far too impulsive and reckless and... *maddening*," he repeated, just in case his father wasn't certain where he stood on the matter.

George Croft sat back and rested a hand on the side of the curricle, tapping his fingers to an unheard tune. "Then you'd want to avoid a young woman like that in order to focus on more suitable candidates."

"Oh, don't worry," he said with a derisive laugh. "She ensures we are never seen at the same function, if at all possible. In fact, since her debut—a full year ago, mind you—we've only met by chance three times." *The stray bonnet in the park, the disaster in the parlor, the blunder in the conservatory...* hmm. Had it really only been three times? The fact that it *seemed* like a greater number of encounters bespoke of how ill suited they were, no doubt.

"And how do you think she manages to avoid you all the time?" his father asked.

Griffin gave the reins a snap, pushing the horses into a trot down the park path. "Do you know she admitted to having me watched for the purpose of avoiding me?" Ludicrous. It irritated him to think that she cared whether or not the *ton* saw them attend the same function.

"Odd, but likely she has her reasons," his father mused, his fingers still tapping. "Though it seems a man wouldn't want such a woman to have the upper hand all the time. In fact, it might even serve her right—give her a taste of her own medicine, to my way of thinking—if she thought you were attending one event, when you actually intended to go to another. Just as a way to even the score."

Griffin found himself nodding, pleased with the idea of getting the better of Delaney McFarland. Perhaps surprising her at the Dorset ball had whetted his appetite. "You know, Father, you might be on to something."

For the past two mornings, Delaney had received a missive from Montwood, informing her of his regrets. Yesterday it had been a forgotten previous engagement, and today he'd been called out of town for the remainder of the week. Yet even on paper, he exuded charm, stating how much he looked forward to their ride in the park, very soon.

Delaney did her best not to feel slighted, but her inner flame was still a fragile, flickering little thing. She'd looked forward to an outing with Montwood, though for an entirely different reason than her original purpose. Now, she wanted to ride in the park—preferably in an open barouche—solely to put Griffin Croft in his place. The gall of *that man*, believing he had the right to dictate her actions! She couldn't wait to show him what she thought of his opinion.

Unfortunately, today's missive kept her spirits low. That was, until she remembered that she was meeting her friends for their needlework circle. Surely an afternoon with her friends was just the thing to lift her spirits.

The idea made her feel better, and she mounted the servants' stairs to the attic.

Tillie, a wholesome-faced young woman with a tidy knot of corn silk hair, opened the door. "Almost done, miss," Tillie said with a needle clamped between her lips and a scrap of muslin in her grasp.

Because of Gil McFarland's temper, a considerable number of Delaney's personal maids had come and gone in this house. Many of the more timid ones had left their notices at the door and vanished in the middle of the night. Of course, Delaney knew her impossible hair had played a part in that too. After all, no self-respecting lady's maid would want to take credit for her untamable mess of curls. Which left Tillie, who'd never trained a day as a maid. Actually, she'd worked in the kitchen.

When Delaney's previous maid had quit, taking her younger brother—the McFarlands' former tiger—with her the night before her debut, Delaney had asked the staff if there were any volunteers to fill the vacant position. Tillie had been the only one brave enough to step forward, sealing her fate with "I'll give it a go." In her kitchen experience, she'd come up with an olive-oil-and-lavender concoction that had helped tame some of the more fearsome tangles that night.

To this day, Tillie knew nothing about either hair or fashion. She couldn't tell sarcenet from paramatta. Even so, her maid's worth was far above and beyond all those who'd come before her—and all because Delaney didn't have the patience for needlework.

Needlework didn't require enough movement, not to mention, all that *sitting....Frankly, the idea of sitting still for longer than absolutely necessary sets my teeth on edge.* Nonetheless, she really liked spending time with her friends, and she couldn't very well sit there with nothing in her lap while everyone else kept punching a needle through fabric as they chatted away.

So when she'd watched Tillie's quick needlework that first week, Delaney had been inspired. She'd made a bargain with her maid: if Tillie could produce a partially finished bit of needlework for her twice a week and keep it a secret, then Delaney would style her own hair. Needless to say, the former kitchen maid had leapt at the chance.

Now, a year later, Tillie wrapped up the bundle of muslin that Delaney would take to Penelope Weatherstone's parlor this afternoon.

"I used a bit of wax to mark the space of your next stitches," Tillie said, her mouth turning into a frown. "It's no more than a row of half stitches. Just take it slow."

In the past year, her maid had expressed disappointment over several projects Delaney had managed to ruin because of her desire to rush. She'd ended up with holes in more than half of them.

"Not to worry. This one will turn out fine." Delaney always said that. Still, in her own defense, she had been right some of those times. More or less.

Tillie sighed. "I'm almost finished adding the extra flounce to your gown for the theater this evening."

"Oh, blast!" A sudden realization struck her hard. It wasn't that she'd forgotten about her plans for the theater. No. It was that she remembered her father's box was situated directly below the Earl of Marlbrook's.

No doubt Griffin Croft would be there. She didn't know if she could bear to see the man who'd kissed her solely to prove a point. For an all too brief moment, she'd actually imagined he'd been swept away in the moment. She should have known better.

There was only one thing she could do. She needed to go shopping.

Also... "Tillie, is there time to add one more flounce?"

Shopping with Calliope and the twins had drained every last ounce of energy from Griffin. He'd barely returned from his outing with Father when they'd dragged him into the waiting carriage, eager for new bonnets and gloves. He hadn't even had a chance to eat.

Now, hours later and with packages piled high beside the driver, his lack of sustenance was taking its toll. He yawned and leaned back against the squabs, tilting his beaver hat over one eye.

One of his sisters called for the driver to stop. Again.

This day would never end. In fact, he still had to escort the lot of them to the theater this evening. "There couldn't possibly be a shop you've not yet explored."

Phoebe grinned. "Bree McFarland mentioned that she frequents Haversham's in favor of Forrester's and, since we are passing by, I thought it the perfect time to see why she prefers it."

"Likely the reason is because this shop is closer to Danbury Lane, where she and her sister live," he said, hoping against hope that it was enough to convince her to continue homeward.

"How do *you* know where the Misses McFarland live?" Asteria grinned broadly.

He cursed himself for supplying any sort of encouragement. "The longer you are in society, the sooner you'll learn where everyone lives."

"And speaking of Miss McFarland, I believe that is Bree's sister outside of Haversham's this very moment," Calliope offered. Her sly, sideways smile told him that she knew very well what she was doing.

He was glad for only one thing—that the betraying leap of his pulse was not observed by the three of them.

The kiss in the Dorsets' conservatory had been a mistake, an undisciplined impulse, to which he'd never given in before. Yet he couldn't deny that the memory of it kept stirring inside him like a bubbling cauldron. Perhaps Miss McFarland had been right all along in her attempts to avoid him.

Still, knowing she'd been doing so on purpose—even employing a spy—irked him to no end. Therefore, when the coach stopped, he quickly exited the carriage, handing his sisters out one by one. Anticipation filled him.

Once they were all out, Asteria linked her arm inside his, with Calliope and Phoebe leading the way. "Your sluggishness this afternoon seems to have evaporated, brother."

"I'm merely anxious to end the outing and have a moment's peace," he said, gazing ahead. From the looks of it, Miss McFarland had left the shop too quickly and was now being hailed by a store clerk, who hoisted her package in the air by the strings.

With every step, Griffin kept his eyes on the tilt of her sea-foam green bonnet, a length of silver ribbon left untied and flitting about in the breeze. She wore a short jacket with a stiff collar in the same hue and a row of tiny buttons down the front.

Those buttons stirred him anew, causing him to imagine unfastening them, enticing him to expose the delectably small firm mounds of her bosom beneath the layer of pale muslin she wore today. After their kiss, he'd memorized nearly every fine distinction of her form. Because of that, he knew she didn't wear stays, which made those buttons almost irresistible.

"Miss McFarland," Calliope greeted. "What a pleasure it was to spot you from our carriage. My brother insisted we stop and bid you good afternoon."

The bonnet turned. The remains of a furrowed brow quickly dissolved as a seemingly practiced smile lifted the corners of her mouth. Only the barest hint of surprise slipped out by way of the soundless exclamation on her lips, but he saw it all the same. Those violet eyes skimmed across his sisters, one after the other, and then hesitated for the barest part of a second on his. Two dots of pale pink tinged her cheeks as she returned her gaze to the eldest of his sisters.

The clerk bowed and disappeared back into the store.

"Miss Croft. What a flattering thing to say," Miss McFarland replied easily, in no way revealing the fact that she'd looked to be in a terrible rush only a moment ago. "Although…I have a younger sister as well, and I know that siblings breakfast on bowls of mischief each morning. It's far more likely that you are here to see if *my* Haversham's is superior to *your* Forrester's—which it is, of course, in every way," she ended with a grin that hinted at a dimple in her left cheek. When she reached up to tuck a flyaway auburn tendril behind her ear, his view was obscured.

He would've liked to have seen the dimple again to be sure it existed. She seldom smiled in his presence—not with genuine amusement instead of with obligatory social politesse—and he felt that he'd just unearthed a great secret.

"You are too clever, Miss McFarland," Phoebe said. "Only Griffin ever calls us out for our penchant for mischief. You must have like minds."

"More likely, our siblings are quite similar," she said smoothly, doing a better job at dissuading his sister's evident matchmaking scheme than he'd done. "And speaking of siblings, I'm certain mine would enjoy a visit from each of you, now that you are on this side of town."

Asteria nearly clapped with glee. "That is a nice trick, inviting us to call when my brother could hardly refuse."

"Our carriage is at your disposal," Griffin offered, unable to keep the smirk from his lips. There'd be no avoiding him this time. Her spy could not have prepared her for this circumstance. "My sisters and I will simply return to Haversham's on a future outing."

Pink brushed Delaney's cheeks again as she drew in a breath. "Apparently, my cleverness has already abandoned me. Truly, I was merely doing a service for my sister. She enjoys your company immensely. I never intended to imply she'd confided an interest in having your brother pay a call on her."

"Then he could call on *you* while we visit your sister," Phoebe said with a glint of triumph.

Griffin felt his own triumph stir and wondered what it would be like to pay a call on Delaney McFarland. Would they sit across from each other, engaging in courteous conversation while pretending that the kiss in the Dorsets' conservatory never happened? Or would she again confess to a strange crackling sensation beneath her skin and feeling as if she was about to catch fire?

"Oh dear. I've done it again." Miss McFarland's gaze was apologetic until it glanced across his. Then, he could have sworn it turned to challenge. "You see, I will not be at home for visitors. I have another engagement I must attend."

His sisters exchanged looks of disappointment. If it weren't for his ire suddenly being piqued at knowing that this was her way of avoiding him, he might have felt disappointment as well.

Asteria stepped forward. "But you will be at the theater tonight, will you not?"

She opened her mouth but closed it directly, apparently at a loss for an excuse. Now, it was his turn to gloat. Before he could say something to incite her even more, however, the door of Haversham's jingled again and out stepped Miss Mallory.

"Elena, you are just in time." Miss McFarland sidled up to her instantly. "I'm sure you must know the Misses Phoebe and Asteria Croft. And of course, you're acquainted with Mr. Croft," she said nearly inaudibly. "But have you met Miss Calliope Croft?"

Miss Mallory was only too delighted to make the new acquaintance.

Griffin watched as Miss McFarland's gaze turned calculating. Even though they'd barely spoken, he felt as if he knew each of her looks. A sense of certainty filled him. In fact, he knew what was coming before she opened her mouth to speak.

"Only moments ago, Miss Mallory and I were conversing of her desire to attend the theater this evening," Miss McFarland said, that small dimple taunting him. "Alas, my father's box only seats six, and those are all taken. I believe your uncle's box, though, is quite large, is it not, Mr. Croft?"

Mis-ter Croft. He could almost taste her syllables on his tongue.

"It is." He clenched his teeth together in a grin. Obligated now, he looked from Miss McFarland to her cousin. "Miss Mallory, it would be my great honor if you would accompany my sisters and me."

When Elena Mallory's pinched face opened into a grin, he felt as if he were seeing a direct descendant of ancient dragons. It appeared as though she possessed two rows of jagged tips sharp enough to bite through leather. He was suddenly quite nervous for his boots.

Miss Mallory tittered, a high-pitched whinny issuing through her nose and piercing his ears. "I'd be delighted, sir."

"Lovely," Miss McFarland said and aimed a rather cheeky wink in his direction when no one else was looking. The air rushed out of Griffin so suddenly that he felt as if he'd taken a punch to the stomach. The wink took him off guard. And yet, already, he wanted her to do it again.

Then, too quickly, she made her excuses, leaving them in her cousin's care. And to Griffin, she'd somehow taken away the vibrancy of the afternoon at the same time.

A mad urge to follow her trampled through him, but he remained on the walking path outside the shop. The shifting of his boots on the ground was the only indication that he wrestled for a moment.

"Allow us to drop you at home, Miss Mallory," Calliope offered, gesturing to the carriage. "It is fortunate for us that our brother knows *everyone's* address, so we needn't ask for it."

The eldest of his sisters cast him an impish smile.

He hated that he was about to fall into her trap, and he blamed Miss McFarland for all of it. Especially for unsettling him. When he saw the culprit this evening, he would be sure to pay her back in kind.

CHAPTER SIX

"I'm truly going to be ill, Griffin," Asteria said as he escorted her below stairs during intermission. Calliope and Phoebe had stayed behind. He suspected, however, that the younger of the twins was speaking for all of his sisters. "Miss Mallory is in our box this instant, leaning across to Lady Amherst—one of the most notorious gossips in all of London—making claims against Lord Rathburn and Miss Danvers. You should march up there this instant and come to her defense."

"I hardly know Miss Danvers. Such an act by a gentleman who is not amongst her or her family's coterie might incur more damage than assistance." Although, he could see his sister's point. He needed to put a stop to the gossiping ninny before she sullied someone's reputation.

Miss Mallory's barely veiled innuendo of Rathburn's previous involvement with an actress had been enough for him to clear his throat and mention that his younger sisters were new to the sights and sounds of town. Unfortunately, she hadn't taken the hint. In fact, she'd actually offered to escort the twins to more functions and help him act as chaperone.

He'd had enough. Clearly, a private and very blunt conversation was needed.

"I meant you should come to Miss McFarland's defense." His sister stared at him as if he'd half a brain. "Surely, you've heard the rumors that Miss Mallory is a cousin of hers."

"I have," he admitted and ignored the twinkle of mischief in his sister's blue eyes, as if he'd just been caught raiding the kitchen for gingerbread. "Still, I don't see what that has to do with Lord Rathburn and his betrothed."

"Miss Danvers is a particular friend of Miss McFarland's. Therefore, it stands to reason that Miss Mallory is merely attacking her by way of Miss Danvers's reputation. After all, Phoebe and I have heard from more than one person who remembers the way Miss Mallory stood in the McFarlands' ballroom last year, gloating all throughout the..." She pursed her lips as if searching for a delicate way to put it.

"*Incident,*" he supplied. Oddly, the term sparked a glint of unexpected warmth through him.

"*Incident* sounds much better than *abominable horror,* which is how Phoebe and I refer to it." She nodded in acceptance but gave him the knowing look she'd adopted recently. "It's fortunate that Miss McFarland has a friend in you."

He ignored the comment. "When we return to the box, we'll make a very public exit with Miss Mallory, sending a clear message of intolerance."

"Oh, yes! That will be perfect." She nodded eagerly but then turned thoughtful. "No. That will *not* do. A public exit will cause more people to wonder at the reason, and then Miss Mallory's gossip will only spread faster." Her gloved finger tapped against her chin as she frowned. "She's put us in a terrible predicament. I'm not afraid to say that I do not like her one bit. Although…it was clever of Miss McFarland to put her in your path, pretending disinterest."

"You manage to see pretense where there is none." The only reason a woman would put another woman in a gentleman's path would be to ensure that he understood she had no interest. Griffin used the same tactic when introduced to a debutante with whom he didn't want to dance—he simply introduced her to the nearest gentleman and quickly took his leave. "Not every person's actions are part of a grand plot, as you and Phoebe seem to imagine."

"Oh, but you are wrong. Phoebe and I have a chart that helps us." She paused and looked askance at him. "Well, the reason isn't important. You'll have to trust me."

He knew by now that it was better not to ask.

Just then, he saw Miss McFarland and her friend Miss Wakefield turn the corner from the refreshment area, heads bent together as they whispered. Their collective frowns told him well enough that they'd heard Miss Mallory's claims. A fresh sweep of irritation at the young woman in his uncle's box fell over him.

Griffin escorted his sister directly in their paths and greeted both of them in turn. "How are you enjoying the play?"

The two exchanged a look.

Miss McFarland's expression transformed into one of fiery determination in the quick jut of her shapely chin. A gleam flared in her gaze. "Better, now that we have spent *all this time* conversing with our good friends, Miss Danvers and Lord Rathburn," she said, elevating her voice slightly, seemingly so that the few still lingering in the gallery might overhear.

While he'd given her credit for being clever, now he witnessed her devout loyalty as well. He suddenly decided that her friends were most fortunate indeed.

"But I thought...*oh*." It took Asteria a moment to catch on, but she quickly recovered. "When I saw you leave before intermission, I'd wondered if you were off to speak with your friends."

Miss McFarland reached out and squeezed his sister's hand, an affectionate smile on her face. "Yes, and we have great news as well, but it would be wrong of me to boast about it."

"Surely not too boastful," Miss Wakefield chimed in, as if the entire exchange had been rehearsed. "Naturally, it would pain us to conceal our glee for having received an invitation to picnic at Hawthorne Manor."

This was news. There hadn't been a party at Hawthorne Manor in years. From the corner of his eye, he caught sight of the eavesdropping Leticia Cumberland—a particular friend of Lady Amherst's—and quickly knew Miss McFarland's plan would work.

"Although since it is only for the wedding party, it would be wrong to let everyone know. So it will have to be our secret." The moment when Miss McFarland said those words, her gaze met his. A familiar tint of pale pink blended with the freckles on her cheeks.

They shared a secret as well. He inclined his head, trying to ignore the sudden rush of heat. "You honor us with this confidence."

"Might I share this news with my sisters, once I return to the box?" Asteria asked, rather too slyly.

"Of course," Miss Wakefield responded and stepped forward to link arms with her. "Just as I will share the news with my aunt."

Miss McFarland glanced to her retreating friend and his sister, and then to him. She drew in a quick breath. "I must be off as well. Thank you, Mr. Croft, for—"

"Keeping *our*—I mean, *your* secret?" He couldn't help the teasing grin that curled the corners of his mouth. "It was entirely my pleasure, Miss McFarland."

That lush violet gaze narrowed for an instant, and he felt another stab of heat. "I do hope you are enjoying my cousin's company this evening," she said. "I must warn you, however, if she has a cup of punch waiting for you, I would not drink it."

He tucked the odd remark away for the moment since the orchestra went from tuning their instruments to the beginning of the score. "Trying to dissuade any potential interest I might have in another woman, Miss McFarland?" Extending his elbow, he silently offered to escort her to her father's box.

Surprisingly, she accepted. Together, they moved up the stairs behind his sister and Miss Wakefield. With each step, the lavender flounces over Miss McFarland's bodice shimmied, drawing his attention and increasing his desire to explore what lay beneath. He had no idea how such a small bosom could entice him so.

"Hardly," she said, her tone edged with saucy provocation. "I put her in your path solely to bring you misery."

He allowed his gaze to roam over her slender throat, her freckled face, her flaming, unruly hair, not understanding how such a combination could appeal to him.

Yet unaccountably, it did. "Then why the warning?"

"You did my friend a service just now, and I thought it only right to return the favor." She reached up to tuck a curl behind her ear, where two silver combs attempted to keep the mass of auburn curls from tumbling free.

When the lock sprang forward again, this time he reached out and tucked it in place. The intimacy of the gesture was not lost on Miss McFarland. She looked up at him, eyes wide.

Griffin abruptly lowered his hand. "Sometimes a firmer hand is all that's needed," he mumbled by way of an excuse.

The curl bounced free again. A look of firm resolve replaced the shock in her violet petal irises. "And some things rebel against any type of restraint, Mr. Croft."

Without another word, she turned to join her friend under the dome of the rotunda, not realizing the havoc clambering through him whenever she was near.

CHAPTER SEVEN

"Father, do you think I could wear Mother's sapphire necklace to the Moncrieff ball tomorrow evening?" Bree asked before taking a dainty bite of the braised lamb on her plate. "I'm told the color would complement my eyes."

Sitting across the dining room table from Delaney, Bree seemed oblivious to the way the mention of their mother only brought her absence into sharp focus. Their father's hand stilled briefly before he resumed cutting into his chop.

With a terse nod, he said, "You may. But only if your sister isn't planning on it for herself. Needless to say, there's no reason to give her an excuse to run off to the jewelers tomorrow and charge up my account."

Delaney didn't bother to be offended by the comment. The truth was, she'd been known to make that excuse. She still felt she should protest, however, strictly as a matter of principle.

But before she could say a word, Bree added, with a different sort of bite, "She already has her own jewels that match her eyes."

Instantly, she knew the reason behind it. Their mother had given Delaney her necklace shortly before her debut. Even though their mother had been absent for both of their debuts, Bree had yet to receive a gift for hers. Never once, until this moment, had the thought occurred to Delaney.

Thinking back to the promise she'd made to their mother, Delaney felt ashamed for not having taken better care of her sister's feelings through all this. Not to mention, there was a great deal of anger toward both of their parents for creating all this idiocy in the first place.

"Mother's sapphires suit your coloring perfectly," Delaney said to her sister as a small token of kindness.

"Then it's settled," their father said. The terseness of his words indicated that the subject was closed, and further mention of their mother or her jewelry would not be welcome.

They ate in silence for a time. Gil McFarland opened his embossed gold watch and placed it on the glossed teak table beside his silverware. Delaney despised the sight of it. Without a word, he made it patently clear that he would rather be anywhere else than with his daughters at dinner.

He usually spent time at his club or working late hours in his study, pouring over account ledgers and managing his many estates. As a second son, he took great pride in exceeding both his father's and elder brother's income.

"Did you read the letter I left on your desk about Mr. Harrison and the children of Warthall Place?" Delaney asked, knowing full well he couldn't escape her this time.

"I did."

"And?" She dared to hope he would use some of his wealth to aid Mr. Harrison in expanding Warthall Place.

Her father expelled a breath. "The answer is the same as it was the first seven times you asked."

When Delaney had first met Mr. Harrison and heard him utter the words, "Everyone deserves to have a sense of purpose," she'd felt an instant connection. All her life, she'd known her purpose was to marry advantageously, as her mother had done. In other words, it never mattered who she was as a person, only the money mattered. Yet the idea that marriage was her only purpose left her feeling empty. Or at least, until she met Mr. Harrison and realized that she could do some good for someone else, especially through such a marriage to Montwood. As soon as he agreed to her terms…

"Mr. Harrison visits workhouses and orphanages," she continued, "in search of children who normally aren't given many opportunities because of misfortune."

"Delaney," her father warned, his knuckles whitening on the grip he had around his fork and knife.

"These children are seen as a burden because of a missing limb or lack of sight, instead of being given a true objective and the means to support themselves for the rest of their days—"

"Enough!" His silverware clattered against the plate.

She knew she shouldn't have pushed him, but she had as little success in keeping her mouth still as she had the rest of her person. In fact, she was probably the reason her father hated these weekly dinners. After all, he'd married so that someone else could see to the messy business of raising the children and keeping up appearances—that, and for her mother's fortune, of course. He never wanted to be bothered with his children.

Yet as a member of the *ton* and having two daughters of marriageable age, he would have to be bothered at some point. Since Mother had gone away, more often than not in these past years he'd been forced to hire a chaperone to remove the burden of having to spend any more time than absolutely necessary with his daughters.

Unfortunately for him, even the most reputable decorum instructor earned a night off once a week.

"Miss Pursglove informs me that you attended a picnic this afternoon." Her father directed this to Delaney, even though he stared at his watch with each word.

"Yes, sir." While she wanted to go into detail and share the wonder and magnificence she'd seen at Hawthorne Manor, she couldn't bear to see him react in his typical manner. His fork would still over his plate. He'd release an exhausted breath through his nostrils. And in his gaze, she would see how desperately he wanted to quit the room.

She despised that look, and even more, hated the tears that had followed when she was alone in her room. Too many times, she'd let anger cloud the hurt she felt. Too many times, she'd been the one to leap up from the table in her rage, toppling her chair behind her as *she'd* quit the room before he could.

Her mother always said she was too much like her father in that regard.

Elspeth McFarland had often told her husband that he needed to put his temper through a sieve before he put the pot on the flame. Delaney supposed the same was true for her. After all, hadn't that been one of the reasons her parents had made her wait until she was twenty before her debut?

In all fairness, she credited her mother's frequent absence for teaching her to rein in the more volcanic aspects of her personality. Father, too, didn't shout as much these days. Strangely enough, his more temperate and distant persona unsettled her more than the boisterous father she'd always known.

In certain ways, he was still the same. Gil McFarland was a man who saw only two solutions to any problem—throw money at it, or yell at it. Worst of all, instead of yelling at her for horrendously ruining her chances for a suitable match and forever staining her name, as well as the family's, her father had added an enormous sum of money to her already generous dowry and summarily closed the accounting ledger—both on the matter of her dowry and on their relationship. He never yelled once about *the incident.*

Sometimes, Delaney wished he would.

At least then she could yell right back. And maybe find out why her parents had so easily abandoned her.

She set her knife and fork down across her plate, her appetite gone. There were certain things she couldn't bear to ask, because he might actually give her an answer. "Have you heard from Mother?" she asked instead.

Her father's fork paused over his plate. He exhaled through his nostrils and glanced at the watch. "Just today, as a matter of fact." He set his fork down, wiped his mouth, and laid his napkin over his plate. Instantly, a footman rushed over and removed it. "It seems your aunt's health is much improved."

"Did she inquire about us?" Bree asked before he could push away from the table. "Did she wonder how my first Season is progressing?"

Delaney looked across the table at her sister, who was so much like their mother in her coloring and demeanor. Golden locks curled to frame her face. Neither blemish nor freckle ever marred her creamy complexion. Her regal features had already gained her recognition as one of the premier beauties of the Season. And yet, just now, on the surface of her blue gaze, Delaney saw so much hope and longing that it gave her heart a sharp pinch.

She'd felt that way too, when their mother was absent for her first Season.

"Of course your mother inquired," Gil McFarland answered, glancing first to his watch and then to the door. He set his hands on the edge of the table.

Bree wasn't finished. "And what did you tell her?" She still had years before she understood that their parents' marriage had never been anything other than a monetary transaction. Which begged the question—were they doomed to share their mother's fate?

This time, their father stood. "I explained that you are both in excellent health." He strode out of the room, gesturing for the footman to close the door behind him.

Delaney saw her sister's eyes glisten with unshed tears as she stared at the door. Though Delaney hated to admit it to herself, she'd held on to a wild, girlish dream that their parents had once been passionately in love too. The more she matured, however, the more she realized the truth: theirs had never been a love match.

Sometimes she wondered if the same realization had occurred to her mother and if that was the reason she often went away to tend to a sick relative. After all, how many ill children could Aunt Charlotte possibly have?

"I imagine she'll return soon," Delaney offered.

Bree regarded her with a skeptical sniff. "She didn't for your debut."

"Yes. Well, if you'll recall, I'd disgraced the family name at mine. For her to rush back on my account would have made it a bigger ordeal than it was." At least, that's what Delaney had told herself. It had been the only way to keep from succumbing to the loneliness she'd felt without her mother to see her through the worst trial of her life. "One day, you'll thank me for lowering society's expectations in order for you to make a grand debut."

Her sister's watery gaze swiftly transformed to sharp daggers, letting her know that the comment was exactly the right thing to say to draw Bree away from a bout of melancholy. "And one day, I'll marry a duke and beg him to allow my spinster sister to live with us in order to care for his slobbering hunting hounds."

Delaney bit back a grin. "It's a good thing you're looking for a duke who doesn't mind slobber. Therefore, your tendency to drool will never be an issue for marital discord."

Delaney ducked in time to miss the fork launched at her head. Perhaps they were more alike than she'd thought. Oddly enough, the idea made her laugh. Heaven help the *ton* if that were true.

Griffin wiped sweat from his brow with the back of his hand. "What say you, Everhart? Man enough for another beating?"

"The cut on your lip states quite clearly which one of is receiving the beating," Gabriel Ludlow, Viscount Everhart, grinned, his teeth outlined in his own blood. "How will you manage to find a bride when your face is mangled? It isn't as if you've charm on your side."

The taunting was typical for a boxing saloon and even more typical between Everhart and Griffin, as they partnered regularly. They were not necessarily friends, though they *were* of equal height, strength, and reach. While his opponent might be lighter on his feet, Griffin possessed more bulk in his shoulders.

"True," Griffin said, approaching the center of the ring, shoulders forward, fists at the ready. "However, some of us do not need charm because we have other *substantial* attributes to offer. Pity for you, I suppose."

That brought Everhart to the center, eyes and teeth flashing. Bare knuckles tapped against Griffin's in a sign that Everhart was ready. Not surprisingly, their exchange had drawn a small crowd, and this was only a practice session. Neither of them performed in bouts but came here for the exercise. Commoners and gentry alike gathered for Jackson's lessons. There was even a little towheaded scamp who came here regularly.

"And here I thought you made *all* the ladies ill, Croft."

His blood boiled in an instant, seething and barely restrained beneath the surface. To bring up Miss McFarland here, besmirching her honor, was unforgivable. He reacted without thinking. His right fist connected hard with Everhart's jaw. His left, with Everhart's abdomen.

Everhart's head snapped to the side as blood sprayed in an arc from his mouth. He staggered back but somehow managed to keep his footing. Bending over, hands on his knees, he spat on the floor. "*Bugger!*"

Griffin was still hot, ready to go again. He danced from one foot to the other. Thus far, he'd been holding back. Ultimately, it would not serve to break the nose of the Duke of Heathcoat's heir. Not to mention, Everhart's grandmother was a veritable dragon. It would be foolish to make an enemy of her.

He never lost his temper. But *damn*, that had felt good.

Everhart straightened, working his jaw back and forth. "I'd no idea, Croft."

"That I could best you any day of the week?" Oh, yes, this rage and aggression felt good. For weeks now, he'd been like a kettle on the boil. It felt even better to release some steam.

Everhart offered a cocky grin in response. "No. That you *have* found yourself a bride, only she can't stand the sight of you."

Griffin took his meaning instantly. The idea of *Miss McFarland* as his *bride* stunned him, causing him to drop his guard for a moment. It was long enough for Everhart to get in an uppercut. Thankfully, the hit was enough to knock sense back into him. Miss McFarland as his bride? Never. They were like fire and water.

After that comment, it was a no-holds-barred battle of brawn. Griffin didn't know if Everhart was wrestling with his own demons, but he knew his own were being exorcised quite thoroughly. His need to find a bride, his father's health, his mother's and sisters' peace of mind, and his great-uncle's constant criticism all weighed on his mind day and night. To top it all off, his thoughts were beleaguered by the calamity he knew as Miss McFarland. For some reason, he couldn't go even half the day without thinking of her and wondering whether or not she was meeting with Montwood.

Now, after another hour of pummeling fists, both he and Everhart were breathing hard. Bent at the waist with hands on their knees, they sized each other up. "Had enough?"

"I'm man enough to realize I've stepped over a line." Everhart grinned and held out his hand. "I won't make that mistake again."

Griffin shook his hand and nodded. He could easily have corrected the misguided assumption, but he wanted to leave the matter alone—for his own sanity's sake. "See that you don't."

In the antechamber, after wiping off the sweat, Griffin donned a fresh a shirt. He was in the process of buttoning his waistcoat when, out of the corner of his eye, he caught sight of the towheaded boy. One couldn't miss the head full of pale curls or even that one sleeve of his jacket fell empty against his side. Griffin had seen enough street urchins with missing limbs that one rarely stood out from another. What did stand out, however, was the quality of his clothes. This was no street urchin.

The lad frequented these practices. In fact, he was present each time Griffin was here. Coincidence? Ten days ago— before the Dorset ball—he would have thought so. Now, prickles of suspicion skittered through him.

Without trying to be obvious, he paid closer attention. The boy wore livery, as if employed by a great household— familiar livery at that. Griffin could have sworn he'd seen that particular combination of green and blue before.

Suddenly, it dawned on him.

It was that of the McFarlands. He nearly laughed aloud. Could this be the illusive *spy* employed by Miss McFarland?

There was only way to find out. "You there, boy. Fetch me that coat," he said with an absent gesture toward the peg on the wall. When the boy in question stood frozen in place, he snapped his fingers. "Make it quick. I've plans for the evening."

Pale curls sprang into motion as the boy darted over to the wall. "This one, sir?"

Griffin nodded, and the boy hurried over. Griffin gave the impression of disinterest, even turning his back on the lad as he attempted to shrug on his coat. Unfortunately, all his recent exercise had increased the girth of his arms and shoulders, turning it into a struggle. "I've seen you here before. Like boxing, do you?"

"Yes, sir. Allow me, sir." The boy brought a stool over and hopped up on it with the agility of an acrobat. He was so nimble with his movements that one would never know he possessed only one arm unless he saw it for himself.

When the coat was in place, Griffin tossed a coin in the air, not surprised that the boy caught it soundly.

"My thanks. I might have been here all night if not for your assistance," Griffin said as he rolled his shoulders. The fit was snug. No doubt he'd rupture another seam before he reached home. He was forever tearing out the stitches in his sleeves. Assuredly, he'd make his tailor a wealthy man by the end of the Season.

"Couldn't have that, sir. You said yourself that you have plans. Couldn't have you late for the…Moncrieff ball?" The boy hopped off the stool. A sly grin slid in place as if the little spy thought to hoodwink Griffin.

"Of course," Griffin confirmed. "It's the only noteworthy function I can think of, unless you can name another."

The boy blinked. "Another, sir?"

"Yes. I'm certain not every member of the *ton* will be crushed together in the Moncrieffs' ballroom."

The boy swallowed, his face going as pale as his curls. "Someone of your ilk wouldn't attend a boring dinner when there's a fancy ball to be had."

Griffin scoffed as if the answer were obvious. "Of course not." *A dinner? Hmm…* He just happened to know that a certain Lord and Lady Bingham were hosting one of their elaborate dinners this very evening. Not only that, but Lord Bingham was a particular friend of Griffin's father's. He wondered, should he happen to stop by on his way home, if he might discover that a certain auburn-haired *miss* was on the guest list.

CHAPTER EIGHT

"I do believe that Lord and Lady Bingham have the most handsome portraits in the hall," Delaney said, eyeing a particular ancestor whose sunken face appeared to have been trampled by a horse hoof shortly before the painter arrived.

Merribeth nodded in agreement as they continued to study Lord Bingham's great-grandfather. "Perhaps if we take a step back."

They did and then exchanged a look.

"We might end up in the next room before it improves," Delaney whispered, not wanting the other guests to overhear.

Merribeth giggled, covering the sound with her gloved hand. "I think it also depends on the artist. I would rather have one whose view of the world was more romantic, I think."

The thought made Delaney laugh too. "With a crown of flowers in your hair and bluebirds flitting about? I believe I know of another person who would want a portrait just like that."

"And who would that be?"

"Mr. Croft's youngest sister," she said, without thinking of the implications. To mention his name, let alone to suggest an acquaintance with his family, would certainly raise questions. The moment she saw the speculative arch of Merribeth's brow, she quickly went on. "Bree and I happened upon the sisters in the park one day, and the youngest was wearing a crown of flowers."

"What are you two tittering about," Penelope asked as she walked up to them on the arm of her husband.

Delaney looked to Merribeth to see if her ploy had worked. Apparently it had, because her friend's attention was diverted by their companions.

"Our own portraits," Merribeth said, amusement brightening her eyes. "I would dress in a flowing gown amidst meadow flowers—though I'm certain it would look out of place beside Mr. Clairmore's. He'll undoubtedly want his portrait to be severe and stately."

"We haven't discussed portraits yet," Penelope said, gazing thoughtfully at Ethan, "although he requested a miniature for his birthday earlier this year."

Mr. Weatherstone exchanged a look with his wife that made Penelope blush. "I keep it in a very important place."

Delaney felt her heart pinch at the sight of her friend, their love for each other so clear it might have been written in lines of poetry across their faces. If it could be said that Penelope fairly glowed on Mr. Weatherstone's arm, then it could also be said that he emitted his own light.

Penelope automatically settled a hand over her stomach. "Even though family portraits are uncommon, I prefer them. We'll be in Surrey by the time the baby arrives. The manor has a splendid array of arched windows that would make a perfect background."

"Aunt Sophie and I are already planning to be there for the event. I'm certain Mr. Clairmore would want to join us by then as well," Merribeth added, beaming in expectation of a proposal any day now. "But what of your portrait, Delaney?"

She thought for a moment, hiding a sudden twinge of sadness at the knowledge that there would be no family portraits in her future. No doubt, hers would hang somewhere beside Montwood's. "Perhaps I'll stand for hours, posed outside Haversham's."

They all laughed, but Delaney knew only hers was forced. Truth be told, she'd been plagued by a bout of melancholy for the past week. Not even shopping had improved her mood.

After careful consideration, she'd realized the problem was that her plan wasn't going as smoothly as she'd hoped. Even though a bargain with Montwood was the perfect solution, she was beginning to doubt herself. Now, a week and a half after their initial conversation, she hoped that he would return to town and pay a call on her in the next few days. Perhaps then she'd feel more like herself.

Just then, the dinner gong in the Binghams' hall rang. Those who'd ventured into the gallery merged with those who'd remained in the parlor. It was at that precise moment that Delaney saw Mr. Croft. And what was worse, he saw her too.

"What is *he* doing here?" Merribeth leaned in to whisper. "I thought his sisters would be attending the Moncrieff ball this evening."

"So did I…" she murmured.

From the dining room doorway, he inclined his head in her direction. She narrowed her eyes. He was here on purpose—the purpose being to unsettle her—she had no doubt. As if reading her thoughts, he flashed a triumphant smirk before disappearing through the door.

"But I don't see his sisters nearby."

Delaney gritted her teeth. Just this afternoon, Buckley had given her confirmation that Mr. Croft was attending the Moncrieff ball. So this must simply be a terrible coincidence. Either that, or he'd deliberately attempted trickery in order to mislead her spy. "Most likely, they are at Moncrieff House with their mother."

The crackling sensation began again, stinging the center of her palms and working up her arms. She tried to calm herself. It would be impossible to avoid him all evening. Then again, the dinner party was rather large. Perhaps her place card was situated far enough from his that it would be as if they were attending separate functions.

Besides, seeing him at the theater last week had caused only the slightest stir. Coupled with the rumor surrounding the picnic at Hawthorne Manor, their interaction had gone unnoticed.

Feeling marginally better, she linked arms with Merribeth. Together, they crossed the threshold and stepped into the Binghams' lavish dining room.

A half dozen chandeliers on golden chains hung over a table that spanned the length of the room. Crystal water glasses and wine goblets refracted the light in pastel prisms that danced over white linen and porcelain chargers rimmed in gold.

Automatically, her gaze sought Mr. Croft, but only in an effort to avoid him, she told herself. Wearing a tailcoat in dark blue and a waistcoat in bronze silk, he stood at the far end of the room. He wore the mail coach knot again, with a diamond pin in the fold that seemed to wink with devilish delight. Above the line of his pristine cravat, he grinned at her.

Delaney squeezed Merribeth's arm as if she were about to drift to sea and her friend was a mooring line. "As long as he sits on his end of the table and I on mine, no one will even notice," Delaney said, her breath airy. Her lungs constricted in that peculiar way she now associated with the apparent dread she felt whenever Mr. Croft was near. Yet when she noticed the way his hand rested on the curved back of the empty seat beside his, a heated shiver rushed over her. "Surely Lady Bingham is too kind to seat us together."

"I'm certain," Merribeth added just before a footman stepped forward to escort her to her place. At a table that seated one hundred guests, not including the lord and lady at either end, ushers were essential.

One by one, the guests were seated. By the time one of the footmen stepped up to escort Delaney, however, she already knew exactly where her place card sat. With each step closer to Mr. Croft's end of the table, she was able to draw less air into her lungs. The crackling that had started at first glance was now a family of tiny flames licking up her arms, making her skin too warm for satin gloves.

"Miss McFarland," he greeted her, inclining his head as she approached. He waved the footman away and held out her chair for her. "What a pleasant surprise."

She kept a smile firmly in place and took her seat. "I suspect this is less than pleasant for one of us and not quite a surprise for the other, Mr. Croft."

He drew in a quick breath, the sound close enough to her ear that she turned her head. In the depths of his gaze, she saw the same churning heat she'd witnessed at the Dorset ball.

Then, in the next instant, he took his own seat and unfolded his napkin with a snap before laying it across his lap. "It just so happens that Lord Bingham is a particular friend of my father's, so my attendance didn't cause much of a stir. After all, I believe your friends, Miss Danvers and Lord Rathburn, were unable to attend and left a void at the table."

She blinked, caught off guard by the seeming ordinariness of his discourse. Yet she knew better. As with all their other exchanges up until now, this felt far too intense for two people who barely knew one another.

"Miss Danvers is ill, though it is not serious." Delaney, Penelope, and Merribeth had called on her earlier to see if she needed comfort. Emma had professed to feeling fine, other than a headache. Delaney imagined the ailment was caused by Emma and Rathburn's fast-approaching wedding.

"If it wouldn't be too awkward for you, please offer my wishes for her swift return to health when next you see her."

"Thank you," she said, staring at him quizzically.

"Here. Allow me." He breeched the *too* slight distance between them to take her napkin. Much as he had with his own, he snapped it open. Then, before she had the presence of mind to object, he laid it across her lap. When she opened her mouth to tell him his gesture was far too forward, she found the words lodged in her throat.

His fingertips skimmed the top of her thigh, just above her knee. The touch was light and gone instantly. Still, she felt her bones turn liquid and a shock of heat radiate from that spot. Then he brushed those same fingertips across his lips. Impossible as it seemed, she felt that too.

The heat within her traveled upward, intensifying by degree.

"Naturally," he continued conversationally, "Lord and Lady Bingham would look to fill a void. I understand Miss Danvers's place was quickly filled by Miss Beatrice Snodgrass of Cheshire. Then, of course, there was the maneuvering of place cards, seating people of similar interests beside one another…"

He rambled on and on, as if he didn't know he'd set fire to her. Oh, but he knew. He had to know. She felt as if the conflagration were on display for the entire room.

"And yet she put us together," she said, her voice clipped with embarrassment.

He grinned, and that diamond pin winked at her again. "I assured her that our interests are quite similar, Miss McFarland."

She had the urge to press her hand against her stomach to *somehow* extinguish the errant flames. Instead, she smoothed the napkin over her lap. "I have no idea what you could mean, Mr. Croft."

He turned away to take a sip of water, just enough to wet his tongue. She found herself pressing her lips together at the sight before she took a sip from her own goblet.

"I'm certain you have some idea." He looked askance at her, his voice low and—if she didn't know better—*hungry*. "Take gingerbread, for example."

She set her glass down and made sure no curious gazes were aimed their way. As she hoped, the other guests were chatting with their table partners. Lady Bingham's reputation for adept management of a seating arrangement appeared every bit deserved. At least…other than seating Delaney beside Griffin, when they were complete opposites. "I hardly consider a preference for spiced cake a common interest."

"Of course it is," he remarked, as if disagreeing with her was as important to him as breathing, "especially if we were to share such a cake in a…*conservatory*, for example." He took another sip from his goblet, but as he did, his gaze dipped to her mouth. This time it lingered until he swallowed. "That would certainly be a common interest."

The heat within her turned liquid, igniting in a rush, like a flame to lamp oil. "I believe you are mistaken, sir."

"Oh?" He looked as if he doubted it. "The Binghams have a conservatory. Perhaps further exploration of this topic is in order."

Did he want to kiss her again? *No.* It couldn't be true. This was only a calculated attempt to unsettle her. Yet as much as she hated to admit it, his attempts were quite effective.

Regardless, she couldn't help but recall how he hadn't wanted to kiss her the first time. That had been another calculated lesson as well. "I cannot imagine what game you are playing."

"I'm merely participating in this game of hide-and-seek *we* are playing, of course," he answered when she returned her attention to him. Briefly, a footman stepped in to pour the wine. After he moved on down the table, Mr. Croft lifted his glass. "For nearly a year, you have sought to avoid me at all cost, while I have recently discovered how much I enjoy it when you fail in your attempts."

Delaney reached for her wine, needing a moment to regain her equilibrium.

But before she could take a drink, he clinked his glass with hers. "I believe the next move is yours, Miss McFarland."

CHAPTER NINE

The following morning, Delaney found Buckley in the kitchen, charming a bun away from the cook.

"I've grown four inches since I first came here a year ago, Mrs. Gawain," he said with a proud smile as he lifted onto his toes. "It's your fair cooking, it is. Imagine how much taller I should grow if I had a mite more. Not even the whole bun but just a bite." When the cook tried to hide her grin, he went on in a rush. "And I didn't want to mention it to you, but I might have seen this one right here knocked to the floor."

"Oh?" Mrs. Gawain set her hands on her hips. "And who'd be knocking it down?"

"No one here," he assured her, and with such innocence that anyone would expect a halo to glint in the sunlight. "But there *was* a mighty wind that blew through the door when I carried out the ash buckets this morning. That could have done it."

Now it was Delaney's turn to hold back a grin. From the doorway, she cleared her throat. "Mrs. Gawain, if you've no need of Buckley at this very moment, I have a task for him."

Buckley, who didn't possess an ounce of shame, looked from her to the cook. "I imagine I'll need my strength."

At that, Mrs. Gawain looked to Delaney and shrugged, as if she couldn't help herself, and then handed Buckley the bun. "Go on with ye now, wee scamp."

The boy followed Delaney out of the kitchen's back door, up the recessed servants' entrance, and to the outer edge of their small walled garden.

Thankfully, there hadn't been any mention in the *Post* that morning, regarding the fact that both she and Mr. Croft had attended the same dinner. Not one mention of her sitting next to him or any reminder of *the incident*. No mention of how inappropriate it had been for him to lay a napkin across her lap. No mention of how frequently he'd bent to whisper to her. And absolutely no mention of *Miss M*—combusting in her chair.

She credited her fortune to Miss Beatrice Snodgrass of Cheshire, who had shyly announced her engagement to Reginald Hargrove during dessert. Now, the *ton's* focus was on the widower and the quiet country *miss*.

At the memory of last night, Delaney still bristled. Especially, when Mr. Croft had withdrawn her chair at the end of dinner but leaned in just enough to incite her temper with one last remark. "Such a pity. I seem to recall Hargrove was quite dissolute. He would have been perfect for your plot." He'd tsked, his breath curling like steam against her cheek. "It seems yours is not the only attractive dowry this Season."

"Yes, miss?" Buckley said, drawing her back to the matter at hand. Seemingly unconcerned at her reason for seeking

him out, he licked the remains of the pastry from his fingertips before wiping them on his breeches.

Delaney tried to be cross with him—she did. In fact, she
even placed her hands on her hips and gave him a scowl of disapproval. But truth be told, she was far too fond of the little
man standing before her.

Dropping her hands to her sides, she shook her head and
let out an exhale. "How certain were you about Mr. Croft's
plans for last evening?"

He straightened his shoulders as if offended. "As certain
as I could be. I heard it from the man himself."

"Directly from Mr. Croft?" This puzzled her. Buckley's
skill at eavesdropping had never failed her before. "Perhaps
you misunderstood. To whom was he conversing?"

"Why, not a soul, miss. He said the words to me."

She gave a start but did her best to hide it. "You spoke
with him?"

"Don't worry, miss. He doesn't suspect a thing. He
thought I was there to watch him box Lord Everhart. It was
a sight to behold," he said, giving a whistle. "Never seen such
a hard fight, except from Tom Spring. *Cor!* They didn't hold
back neither."

Delaney swallowed. She'd heard that the gentlemen
removed their coats, waistcoats, and sometimes even their
shirts during these lessons. An image of Griffin Croft—
sweating, breathing heavy, and wearing nothing more than a
pair of snug breeches—filled her mind and caused a swift tide
of heat to flood her. She fought the urge to fan herself with
her fingertips.

"And so, after the match, you spoke with him."

"Aye. And I helped him on with his coat. It barely fit after the fight." The boy grinned as if he were suffering from a small case of hero worship. Turning, he jabbed his fist in the air as if fighting an unseen opponent. "I wouldn't be surprised if he busted a sleeve loose before he got home."

"Really," she mused. If that were the case, he'd need to see his tailor this morning. And it just so happened she knew the one on Bond Street he frequented. However, first things first. "What exactly did Mr. Croft say about his plans for last evening?"

Buckley lowered his arm and focused on the toe of his shoe burrowing into bits of crushed clay on the path. "He said that he didn't think the Montcrieffs could fit the entire *ton* in their ballroom and wondered if there was another event."

She closed her eyes. *He knew.* Somehow Griffin Croft had discovered her spy was Buckley all along. After her confession at the Dorset ball, he'd probably kept close watch on those around him, wondering whom she employed as her spy. *Blast!* She never should have let it slip. After all, the only reason Griffin Croft would ask a boy about society events would be to answer his own suspicions.

"Don't worry," Buckley said quickly. "I assured him that he wouldn't want to go to a boring dinner."

Not unless he had something to prove. And after his throwing down the gauntlet last night, she had something to prove as well.

She stepped forward and ruffled Buckley's hair. "You were quite right. It was a rather boring dinner. Do you know, I've a mind to fix that sleeve of yours," she said, giving the empty sleeve a tug and earning a smile in return. "What would you say to a trip to Bond Street to see a certain tailor and have a jacket that doesn't get snagged or caught between doors?"

Griffin strolled into Thomas & Bailey's on Bond Street and stopped short. He'd know that particular shade of auburn hair anywhere. Not to mention the haphazard way the untamable mess was tied with a blue ribbon at the base of her neck.

He felt a peculiar smile tug at his lips. After the challenge he'd issued last night, he wondered when he would see her next.

With the carriage out front, he'd assumed her father was here, so it was a surprise to see Miss McFarland instead. Women frequenting this shop were usually accompanied by their husbands. This morning, Delaney McFarland was the only woman present, which could account for the look of disapproval from the hawk-nosed clerk. In fact, she was the only customer at the moment, although it was rather early. Most of the *ton* were only waking at this hour.

She turned. Her expression didn't show an ounce of surprise at discovering that he was the one who entered the shop. In fact, the deep violet of her eyes was bright as amethysts. During their previous encounters, he'd determined that her eyes turned this shade when she was angry.

"Mr. Croft, you are here at last," she said with a hint of exasperation, as if he'd kept her waiting for some time. "I simply must have your assistance on this matter."

He removed his hat and bowed, indulging her. "I am ever at your service, Miss McFarland."

It was only then that he noticed the towheaded boy step out from behind her. The lad managed to grin and offer a guilty shrug at the same time. The ruse was up. Apparently, Miss McFarland no longer felt the need to hide her spy.

She held a small jacket aloft. Since it had one sleeve cuff pinned to the shoulder, he knew it belonged to the boy beside her. "Mr. Simms is in need of a tailored jacket, one that would allow him more freedom of movement. However, I cannot seem to appeal to this gentleman's"—she shook the jacket at the clerk—"sense of rightness *or* his pocketbook."

"Thomas & Bailey's is a reputable establishment, sir," the clerk said. "We simply do not tailor clothes for the servant class." He sniffed and adjusted his cravat, casting a spurious look down at the boy and Miss McFarland. "Dignity cannot be purchased."

Under normal circumstances, Griffin would have agreed. In this particular instance, the clerk's snobbery rubbed him the wrong way.

"Surely, your sense of *dignity* would allow you to make an exception this once." *Or not*, he guessed by the stony look he received.

Griffin glanced at Miss McFarland and the boy. The latter looked up at him as if he'd just left Mount Olympus and could smite the clerk on the spot. Beside him, Miss McFarland's nostrils flared as she glared across the counter. *Now, if looks could smite...*

"Perhaps Miss McFarland's maid wouldn't think it beneath her," the clerk added. "Or someone from *below* stairs."

Worse and worse. Griffin could feel waves of heat rise from Miss McFarland. With the light coming in through the shop's window behind her, he could almost see a puff of smoke rise from the top of her hat.

She aimed that fire toward the clerk. "Or perhaps you have a tailor," she suggested. "Or does your tailor have a tailor of his own to see to the more menial tasks? Perhaps *he* should open a shop."

Beside her, the towheaded boy squared his shoulders and took a step between Miss McFarland and the counter, as if daring the clerk to say anything else that would offend his mistress.

The clerk looked from Miss McFarland and down to the boy, adjusting his cravat once again. "Furthermore, only our patrons or gentleman's valets are permitted to step foot into Thomas & Bailey's. Kindly remove your cripple—"

Miss McFarland gasped. Still clutching the jacket, her hands automatically covered the boy's ears as if to protect him. "How dare you!"

Griffin's temper ignited in a flash. Faster than he could draw a breath, he shot forward. Leaning across the counter, he stood nose to nose with the clerk. "You've overstepped. Perhaps you believe your behavior upholds the highest of standards, but you are lower than vermin's offal. You will apologize to the lady and the lad."

Griffin could never tolerate blatant cruelty. The words and that disdainful tone were far too similar to those used when his great-uncle had railed at him, time and time again, when he was a lad. *"Have you no sense, boy? Speak, boy! Speak. Stop tripping over your tongue like a cripple."*

Red-faced and wide-eyed, the clerked stammered out an apology.

Griffin stepped back. "Kindly send my final bill to my address, as I'll be settling my account here."

Without another word, he turned on his heel and walked to the door. Miss McFarland was already there, waiting for him, his hat in her grasp. With the light behind her, he couldn't read her expression. And for some nameless reason, he needed to know what she was thinking right at this very moment.

Young Mr. Simms held the door open. Taking his hat, Griffin also claimed Miss McFarland's hand and escorted her to the sidewalk and her waiting carriage. This time, when he looked at her, the brim of her bonnet shielded her eyes as she bent her head to look down to where he still had possession of her hand. Her small fingers felt so natural, curled into his palm, that he'd hardly noticed. Or perhaps that was the opposite of the truth.

He released her at once. Yet with this fierce energy boiling in his veins and seeking an outlet, he wished he had some other employment for his hands. Perhaps he should look into carrying a cane, something he could grip so he wouldn't think about how her slender shoulders had also fit perfectly into his palms when he'd kissed her in the Dorsets' conservatory.

"You are uncharacteristically quiet, Miss McFarland. Have you nothing to say of the…spectacle I made just now?" He'd lost control. It was unacceptable.

At last, she lifted her gaze. For the first time, he could not name her expression. The identity of this one eluded him. It looked entirely too tender, too full of admiration.

"*Uncharacteristically quiet?* When you know so little of my character?"

"I know enough," he said on a breath and felt his lips curl into a grin in response to hers.

She held his gaze for a fraction longer. "Highly unlikely, Mr. Croft."

Before Miss McFarland could notice how his hands opened and closed at his sides in an almost transparent plea to haul her into his arms, she turned to the boy and gave him a few coins.

"We are leaving here and going to visit your friends," she said. "I cannot, in good conscience, arrive without a parcel of sweets from the shop next door. Make sure to get one for yourself."

"One for now," the lad said, with a particularly sly smile. "Or one for later?"

"If you pay close attention to how you spend it," she said, bending to whisper, "you may have enough for a sweet each day this week. This will be your accounting lesson for the day."

With that, the boy was off like a Knightswold Thoroughbred. But halfway there, he stopped and headed back. His brown gaze flitted from Griffin to Miss McFarland. "Will Mr. Croft be coming with us?"

She began to shake her head, but Griffin spoke first. "Of course."

The boy beamed at him and took off at a run again.

Her expression altered to one with which Griffin was more familiar—*exasperation*. That deliciously small, deceptively generous mouth released a sigh. "You don't even know where we're going."

"It matters little," he said, suddenly conscious of tilting his head slightly in a way that would fit their mouths together perfectly if he were to close the distance between them and then fit his hands around her shoulders, haul her to her toes…

"And why is that, Mr. Croft?"

Those three syllables sent a shudder through him. For a moment, he forgot what he was saying. Abruptly, he straightened his neck as well as his posture. "I…I need an occupation or might very well find myself doing something I should not." *Like kissing you senseless here on Bond Street.*

She glanced toward the shop door as if it had everything to do with the clerk, whom he'd left rather purple in the face. "You surprise me. Until a moment ago, I never would have guessed we were alike in any regard. I thought your aloofness and arrogance meant you are always in control. That every action you take is calculated." She lifted her gaze to his, eyes bright, lips curled in something just shy of mockery. "But now, I know that sometimes even you give in to impulse. I am seeing you in an entirely new light."

The breeze set free four—no, five—untamed auburn locks from her ribbon. They swept forward, the ends dancing in his direction like five fiery arms extending toward him, beckoning him closer to the flames. "This was not the first time I've given in to impulse, as you might recall," he said, his voice low and hoarse, as if a tide of heat had dried his throat. He made sure she saw his gaze dip to her mouth, in case there was any question to which impulse he was referring. "Though perhaps you prefer to believe that action was calculated as well." He thought he'd made himself clear at dinner last night.

Two spots of pink tinged her cheeks as her grin faded. "I don't prefer to think anything. In fact, I don't think about it at all."

Griffin laughed at the absurdity of her lie. Hell, even he'd been lying to himself. "It seems we are more alike than you'd care to admit."

She opened her mouth to reply, but at the same moment, the boy bounded out of the sweet shop, carrying his treasures—two parcels tied with string, one smaller than the other, hanging by his fingers.

"You must have used your coin quite wisely," Miss McFarland said, her smile returning. Griffin even caught a glimpse of the elusive dimple.

"The others'll be agog," he said proudly. "Soon everyone will want to come to work for your father."

She ruffled his pale curls and gently tweaked his ear. "They will not work for sweets, and for now, that is all I can give them."

Until she married, the statement implied. All at once, their previous conversation in the Dorsets' conservatory regarding her need for a husband—*in name only*—rushed to the forefront of his mind.

Did this have something to do with the reason why she was willing to marry a pauper? He wasn't sure, because he didn't even know where they were going. It was apparent by her words that it was a place where one could acquire a new servant. That was all he knew.

With a glance to Miss McFarland and knowing that she was as likely to reveal all her secrets as a pugilist was to have both hands tied behind his back, he decided another tactic was in order. "Mr. Simms, have you ever taken a ride in an open curricle or held the reins?"

The boy's eyes went round as pennies. "*Cor!* No, sir."

"Would you like to?"

Miss McFarland placed a hand on the boy's shoulder before he bounced out of his skin. "Just what are you up to, Mr. Cr—"

"Not a thing," he interrupted before she could complete his torment. "I just imagine it would be simpler for the boy to spy on me if he's in same carriage. That is all." He knew it would be easier for him to question the lad about his mistress as well.

"Buckley is quite resourceful. It would be wrong to underestimate him in any fashion," she said, with such pride in her voice that the statement sparked a bit of admiration in him.

He smiled and touched the brim of his hat. "I've certainly learned my lesson on that account today."

"Oh, but the day isn't over quite yet, Mr. Croft."

CHAPTER TEN

Alone in the carriage, Delaney was confused. Somehow, she'd let Griffin Croft get the better of her. Again. Without a single word of argument, she'd given him leave to take Buckley with him to Warthall Place. There was no telling what her *former* spy was revealing.

She blamed her confusion on the fact that Mr. Croft had surprised her. Outside the shop, a moment ago, he'd simply taken hold of her hand as if it was his right. The audacity of his action had bewildered her enough for her to imagine it gave her pleasure. She'd even felt a kinship with him, admiring the way he'd defended Buckley.

Unfortunately, she would have no one to talk to about it until she saw her friends later that afternoon. Then again, she couldn't very well discuss this with Penelope, Emma, or Merribeth without revealing the sordid quandary in which she found herself—that the one man she'd sworn to avoid until her death was now challenging her to seek him out.

Now, arriving at Warthall Place, Mr. Croft was there in an instant, opening the carriage door. Again, he took her hand whether she wanted him to or not. Much to her ever-increasing astonishment, she wanted him to. Delaney liked the feel of his large hand surrounding hers. His touch was as warm as bath water. Not too hot. Just perfect for a good, long soak. She imagined what it would feel like to slowly sink into his embrace, those hands gliding over her…

She shook herself free of the distraction as she stepped down from the carriage. Feet firmly on the walk outside the tall, narrow stone structure of Warthall Place, she couldn't fathom why her hand was still in his grasp—why he hadn't released her or why she hadn't snatched it back from him.

Taking advantage of her uncharacteristic stillness, Mr. Croft removed his hat and bowed. His gaze raked over her slowly. No doubt, he was taking in her exceedingly wild hair this morning, as well as the lack of flounces of her lavender pelisse. Instead, her garment was rather fitted, with small leaf-like points of fabric gathered over the bodice. As he appeared to notice every one, a thrill washed through her.

When at last he lifted his gaze to hers, a full grin widened his mouth. Surprisingly, his teeth were not perfectly straight. Not perfectly in order. Their slight crookedness seemed to coincide with the glimpses she'd had of the impulsive nature he kept locked inside him. It was a decidedly wicked grin.

She felt her lungs constrict and drew a breath to inflate them again, though it didn't seem to work as long as she kept her gaze on Mr. Croft.

Pulling her hand free, she turned to the driver. "Dorsey, please return to the market and retrieve Tillie and Betsy. I should be finished in an hour." Normally, when she went on these early morning excursions without Bree or Miss

Pursglove, she took Tillie with her. Today, however, Tillie had wanted to go with Betsy to the market, and Delaney
decided to be generous and have the driver drop them off first
before taking her and Buckley to that horrid shop.

With a nod and a flick of the reins, Dorsey set off. Packages in hand, Buckley ran past her without a word and up the
steps to the large lacquered door. Since Mr. Harrison left it
unlatched during the day, he only had to nudge it open with
his shoulder—which left her quite alone and out in the open
with Mr. Croft.

She looked down the street both ways, hoping this
encounter—and the one at the shop earlier—would go unnoticed and not wind up in the *Post*.

Mr. Croft seemed to find her worry amusing, as he, too,
peered down both ends of the street. "Looking for a way to
escape, Miss McFarland? I believe I see a horse cart coming
our way. Perhaps the man driving it is in need of a wife with a
good fortune. Should I hail him, do you think?"

"You make a habit of taking enjoyment in matters which
are no concern of yours."

That grin reappeared, but he did not bother to respond to
her question. "Young Mr. Simms tells me that you are teaching him a trade, and he intends to manage your accounts
when he is older."

She wondered if that was the only bit of information he'd
managed to winkle out of Buckley. "He deserves to have a
sense of purpose as much as anyone else."

"And what is your purpose, hmm? To have everyone
believe that you exist solely to charge up your father's accounts
and make a nuisance of yourself?"

She clenched her fists at her sides and felt her nostrils flare as she drew in a breath. So many scathing comments crowded together on the tip of her tongue that she was left fuming in silence.

He used it to his advantage. "If there is one thing I know about you," he said, his voice low as he took one step closer, "it is that you have a reason for every action you take."

There was no reprimand in his tone but something resembling admiration instead. She hardly knew what to make of it. Then, in that instant, their discourse altered. With his nearness, she felt those crackling flames lick over body. Heat rose from her flesh, blurring the air between them.

She wet her lips. "How can that be true of someone so often accused of being impulsive and reckless?"

"Because you are too quick-witted for your own good. I shudder to think what a mind like yours could do if it were bent on world domination instead of on vexing me." He leaned in ever so slightly and traced the silk piping along the outer edge of her sleeve. The sensation was so sharp, she felt as if her clothes were part of her, connected by nerve and tissue. "No doubt, there would be a special prison for men with sloppy cravats."

Though she wore the finest cambric chemise, it suddenly felt coarse, causing her nipples to pucker and ache. That same sensation traveled lower as well, as if she wore bristly fabric on the inside of her skin. Below her navel, her insides drew up tightly like the cords of a reticule being cinched closed. Looking over his attire, from his *mathematical knot* down to the buttons of his striped waistcoat, she wondered if he were conscious of the way his shirtsleeves felt against his skin, of what *his* shirt would feel like against *her* skin…

"It takes little effort on my part to vex you," she said, hearing a slight tremor in her voice. The same tremor that rushed through her limbs.

"Then I fear your keen mind all the more," he said quietly and without amusement. The lake water in his gaze churned as if a cauldron brewed beneath the surface. Abruptly, he removed his hand from her sleeve, straightened, and took a step back.

As he had during the Binghams' dinner, he swept the tips of his fingers against his lips.

Delaney drew in a breath, off balance by the chaos his gesture wrought within her. She pressed a hand to her stomach, as if to keep those reticule cords from being cinched too tightly. "You were the one who challenged me."

"I beg to differ." He shook his head slowly. "You've been a challenge to me since the moment we met and every meeting since."

The reminder of *the incident* instantly doused the flames within her. She was almost grateful for the reprieve from the heat. Still, she could not pass up the opportunity to scold him. "What a very ungentlemanly remark, Mr. Croft."

"Yes, and there was nothing of a *gentleman* in me when I said it but someone far more primitive," he said but made no apology.

She would have continued the exchange and asked him to clarify his statement, but in the same moment, Mr. Harrison appeared in the open door.

"Miss McFarland," he said with a wrinkly grin that lifted his jowls. His gaze moved from hers to Mr. Croft with the reserved assessment of one who'd spent a lifetime in service. "How kind of you drop by."

She suddenly felt like a guilty child who'd been caught sneaking slippers from her mother's wardrobe. To make sure he didn't have the wrong idea—not that there was a right idea when it came to Mr. Croft—she proceeded up the steps to the door. "Mr. Harrison, you'll be delighted to know that Mr. Croft has taken a particular interest in your mission."

Unable to remove years of being a butler, Mr. Harrison kept his hands to his sides and bowed his head. "Very good, sir."

Inside the incomparably polished, immaculate house, seven young men of varying heights stood in a line near the base of the stairs. Even Buckley filed in—second place from the last, according to his height. And like him, each of the boys had suffered either the loss of a limb, multiple digits, eyesight, or even burns.

As the boys were introduced, Delaney glanced up at Mr. Croft. If he was surprised, he didn't show it. Strangely, she felt nervous. She'd never brought anyone here, not even her closest friends. Bree knew of the place but only by name and by the constant pleas to her father.

Still, Mr. Croft didn't reveal what he was thinking, and it was driving her mad. For some unknown reason, she wanted his approval. But what surprised her most of all was that she wanted him to know that she was more than just a dowry.

Griffin was stunned.

Certainly it wasn't every day one encountered a place like Warthall, or even a retired butler like Mr. Harrison. But what stunned him the most was Miss McFarland. This was not an act of charity for her. He could see it in the way her eyes brightened with determination.

Mr. Harrison walked with a pronounced limp as he escorted them into the parlor. Two of the boys, along with Buckley, were sent off to the kitchen to have a tray of tea prepared, while the others were told to return to their work.

Over the next few minutes, Mr. Harrison went on to explain how this institution had begun. "Many years ago, I encountered Lord Warthall near Saint Giles after he was set upon by ruffians, beaten, and robbed of his purse. Even though I was a lad at the time and passed over because of my clubfoot, I did my best to see the master home. In return, he gave me the chance to prove myself and hired me on here in this very house. Throughout my youth, into adulthood, and even in the later years, I was always offered opportunities to achieve great things." He sat up a little straighter. "I was head butler for this house for forty odd years until His Lordship's passing. And when he left me this house, along with a generous endowment, I wanted to give others the same chance to live a life of purpose."

At that, Griffin looked to Miss McFarland. He wondered about the enigma sitting in the chair beside his. Making sure these children felt a sense of purpose was something for which she lived.

His admiration for her grew by leaps and bounds.

Was this part of her reason for wanting to marry a pauper in name only? Was she afraid that if she married anyone with whom she couldn't strike a bargain, then she wouldn't be permitted to aid Mr. Harrison in his quest?

He mulled over the last thought, feeling a sudden tightness in his gut. By all that was right, a husband took control of his wife's funds and would do with them as he saw fit. Most men of good character would permit their wives an allowance. Of course, there had been quite a few who'd spent their own fortunes only to bleed through their wives' in under a year.

So that begged the question, what would her husband do?

His gut clenched again. Abruptly, Griffin stood and moved to the open parlor door, as if to examine the boys at their tasks across the hall. The truth was, he felt restless. An image of Montwood flashed in his mind. Would the infamously charming rake take her up on her offer for a marriage in name only and two separate addresses? Or would he decide a more intimate agreement should be made? And once the cad spent all of her money and used her body, would he abandon her and their children, forcing her to beg for a place back inside her father's home?

"Mr. Croft!" Miss McFarland hissed as she stepped beside him. "Has the door offended you in any way for you to abuse it so?"

He blinked and looked down. Only now did he notice his white-knuckled grip on the edge of the old door and the faint spider-webbing of the painted wood beneath his thumb. He released it instantly. "I apologize. My thoughts were distracted."

Then, before she could ask, he posed a question to her. "Is *this* the reason you wish to sell your fortune to a pauper by way of marriage? So that you can aid Mr. Harrison? Because there are other ways to achieve your goals." He couldn't help but wonder if Mr. Harrison was using Miss McFarland to get to her father's fortune as well. He felt another rise of temper at the thought. Of course, there was only one way to find out.

She took a step back and straightened her shoulders. "I believe I've already stated that my affairs are no concern of yours."

"Mr. Harrison," he said, raising his voice for the older man, even though he kept his gaze on Miss McFarland. "I admire the work you do here. To me, it seems there are more young men who could also thrive beneath your tutelage."

"Indeed, sir. Though I am only one man. Miss McFarland has made the suggestion that I should take on more and hire a tutor as well."

Griffin waited for him to continue, to explain how funds were needed for such a venture. Then after a moment had passed with no request made, he felt the need to prod Mr. Harrison. "No doubt even the generous stipend left to you by the late Lord Warthall would quickly diminish if that were the case."

Miss McFarland fumed at him, her hair in tangles about her face, her hands fisted to her sides, her small bosom rising and falling with each quick breath. "Stop this at once. I won't have your interference."

Another weighted moment passed without a request for aid. Miss McFarland's irritation faded to a look of embarrassment, telling him far more than she would ever admit.

Griffin stared at her, dumbfounded. "He hasn't even asked for your assistance, has he?"

She looked askance at Mr. Harrison, who politely averted his gaze and walked over to the mantel to adjust the time on the clock. "You don't understand how greatly he's improved their circumstances. He's found them abandoned on the streets, thrown out of orphanages, confined to workhouses." She closed her eyes and shook her head, her anger falling away. "There are so many others. So many who need one single chance to prove themselves."

Suddenly, Griffin realized what this meant to her. He also understood why she'd warned him not to underestimate her young Mr. Simms. Delaney McFarland saw herself as someone who wanted one single chance of her own.

Something stronger than admiration stirred within him, but he did not name it.

When she opened her eyes, she speared him with their intensity. "And there are girls, so many girls too. Of course, another school would have to be started…" She gestured to the man across the room. "Mr. Harrison knows a former housekeeper who would be perfect."

"In a separate house, of course," Mr. Harrison said quickly as he approached. "Naturally, as I've explained to Miss McFarland, this is an enormous undertaking. Not to mention, I cannot guarantee how long I'll be able to continue to be of service."

The man had spent his life in service and likely would do until his dying day. Griffin felt humbled to be in the presence of such devotion and ashamed at what his first assumption had been. "I see why Miss McFarland has taken to carrying your banner, sir."

Mr. Harrison's jowls lifted, and he cast an affectionate glance to the woman in question. "Miss McFarland is a true gem."

A day ago, that statement would have made him question the sanity of the speaker. But today, he was inclined to agree. For the first time since their acquaintance, he began to wonder if—

"Hand it over, Maxwell! I'll carry the tea tray." One of the boys whom Mr. Harrison had introduced as Geoffrey pulled hard on the opposite side of a glossy wooden tray, overladen with a large porcelain teapot, several cups and saucers, and a basket of scones.

"Just because I'm blind"—the other boy pulled back—"doesn't mean you can stop me from excelling at my duties."

"Boys! See here," Mr. Harrison said, limping forward.

Griffin stepped into the hall as well, hoping to prevent a catastrophe.

"Your duties are to fill the cupboards and play the violin," Geoffrey huffed with another yank. "Not...to...carry...the—"

Suddenly, the tray flew from Maxwell's hands as Geoffrey stumbled back. Plates, cups, saucers, scones, and the porcelain teapot lifted in the air and hovered for one infinitesimal moment.

Mr. Harrison caught the tray. Miss McFarland pulled Maxwell back and covered his head with her hands. And Griffin reached out to save what he could. He managed to take the neat stack of saucers in one hand. With the other, he attempted the teapot, catching the base of it in the palm of his hand. But it slipped from his glove and toppled toward him.

The lid flew off the top. Tea shot out in an arc of amber liquid flecked with leaves. Somehow, he hooked a thumb into the handle—at the precise moment the scalding liquid drenched the front of his buff breeches. He hissed in pain, biting back an oath.

"Mr. Croft!" Miss McFarland covered her mouth with a hand, presumably to keep her laugh from bubbling out. However, her indelicate snort gave her away.

Just then, Buckley reappeared. With a peppermint stick hanging from the corner of his mouth, he took in the carnage of shattered teacups, crumbled scones, and a deluge of tea. "*Cor!* What a right proper disaster!"

Ah yes, Griffin thought. He should have known it was bound to happen.

CHAPTER ELEVEN

A week before Emma and Rathburn's wedding, Delaney stood in a jewelry shop, bartering over a silver platter.

"As you can see, the scrollwork is quite unique," the bearded shopkeeper said with a flourish of his hand.

Just as she opened her mouth to tell him that she'd seen three other platters with the same scrollwork, she was interrupted by tap on her shoulder. Turning, she found Miss Pursglove scowling in disapproval.

"I must object once more, Miss McFarland," Miss Pursglove said with an uptight sniff. "Surely your father's man would be a better applicant for this task."

Miss Pursglove, Bree, and Elena Mallory were all attending this morning's errand. Miss Pursglove had professed to needing assurance that the gift was a "proper representation of Mr. McFarland's station." Bree had come because Miss Pursglove had told her to do so. And dear cousin Elena had tagged along in order to be the first person who knew what gift the McFarlands were giving Viscount and Viscountess Rathburn.

Some days, the joys of Delaney's existence were simply *too plentiful.*

Even so, this experience was innumerably better than the one she'd had at Thomas & Bailey's five days ago. Then again, there was one person in particular whom she wouldn't mind seeing walk through the door. Not that she'd given Griffin Croft much thought. Or *ever* caught herself wondering if he would suddenly appear at one of her social engagements these past few days.

And never once would she admit to feeling disappointment when he hadn't.

"Father's man is a coward. He doesn't know the first thing about haggling." Delaney gave her own sniff. "It's an art form."

Miss Pursglove shuddered and looked askance at the shopkeeper. "*Haggling* is such a vulgar term, Miss McFarland. Perhaps you could simply purchase the platter, and we could be on our way."

Delaney turned away from her decorum instructor and met the shopkeeper's gaze. "Where were we, Mr. Aramant?"

His cheeks lifted in a grin that seemed to give the ends of his mustachio a slight curl. "Did you know my jewelry is all one of a kind? This particular brooch comes from the farthest reaches of Africa." From the glass case between them, he withdrew a rather large bird of paradise, faceted with innumerable multicolored gemstones.

It was, quite possibly, the most hideous piece of jewelry she'd ever seen. It was absolutely perfect for Miss Pursglove... as a parting gift. *What a lovely thought.* "I imagine the cost of the platter would reduce considerably if one purchased such an astounding brooch."

Mr. Aramant's eyes twinkled. "Perhaps."

"And I also imagine that the engraving would be free," Delaney said with her own smile when the shopkeeper nodded in agreement. Bartering like this always gave her such a sense of satisfaction.

In the next few moments, she wrote out the date of Emma's wedding to have it engraved in the center of the silver platter. When the shopkeeper disappeared into the backroom, she overheard Elena speaking with Bree near the case of cameos.

"It's so fortunate that you've received a voucher for Almack's. I received mine as well," Elena said, preening as she cast a glance in Delaney's direction. "It's matter of pride to be hand-selected by the matrons of society. As you know, not *everyone* earns a voucher."

It was true. Because of the incident, Delaney was practically guaranteed to *never* receive a voucher. And they all knew it. While she usually didn't let society's scorn wound her, with this one thing she'd always felt embarrassed. Just once, she would have liked to attend Almack's. And perhaps dance with Griffin Croft.

"Oh, dear me," Elena offered to Delaney with a false show of concern. "I'd forgotten that you never received yours. Whatever will you do this evening while your sister and I are waltzing? I've heard that Viscount Everhart will be in attendance, not to mention a certain Mr. Croft. It is said that he's closer than ever to becoming the Earl of Marlbrook."

Delaney bristled at the comment. She clearly remembered what he'd mentioned at her debut—that his father was *much more than a gateway to an earldom.* "Would Mr. Croft enjoy knowing that the demise of his beloved father causes you no end of delight?"

Even Miss Pursglove tsked.

"That isn't what I meant," her cousin claimed, her cheeks blotched with embarrassment. Glaring back, she pressed her lips together until they were rimmed with white. "How odd that you would come to his defense. I was nearly ready to discount a rumor I'd heard. But now that I think on it, perhaps it's true."

Delaney refused to ask. Surprisingly, Bree held her tongue as well.

Elena wasn't deterred. She turned toward Bree, her expression a mask of excitement. "I heard that your very own sister was spotted with Mr. Croft outside of Thomas & Bailey's, a tailor your father is known to frequent." Her words came out in a stage whisper, as if she wanted to enlighten the whole shop. Thankfully, the four of them were the only ones present.

Miss Pursglove, however, was none too pleased to learn this tidbit of news. "Can this be correct, Miss McFarland? Were you cavorting without a chaperone in the middle of the street? Imagine what your father will say once he learns of this."

"I'd hardly call it *cav*—" she began but was quickly interrupted.

Bree stepped forward, drawing Miss Pursglove's attention. "I'm certain that of all gentlemen, Delaney would avoid Mr. Croft. The rumor is simply unbelievable," she said with a lilting laugh. When their decorum instructor pursed her lips and gave a slight nod, it appeared as if she accepted Bree's statement as fact.

Taken aback at how her sister had come to her aid, Delaney was speechless. Could it be that all the time spent with the Croft sisters had had a positive effect on Bree?

Bree turned back to Elena. "I have it on very good authority that the only person Mr. Croft has paid any particular attention to has been you, dear cousin."

Elena revealed the full spectacle of her smile. "It is true that he escorted me to the theater, little more than ten days ago."

"And I've heard no mention of anyone else he's favored," Bree added in a knowing whisper. Then she looked at Delaney and offered a smile, as if they shared a secret. Whatever it was Bree thought she knew, she was incorrect.

Nonetheless, Delaney felt an affection for her sister that she never had before. Was it possible they could become friends?

Inside his uncle's townhouse, Griffin handed the stoic head butler his hat and gloves. Although the foyer was well lit with early morning rays streaming through the slender windows, the dark hardwood floors and furnishings gave the space an oppressive feel. Every time he came here, he had the sense of being closed in a coffin.

"Lord Marlbrook is in his rooms, Mr. Croft," the butler said with a bow.

Griffin looked up the stairs, dread making his limbs heavy. "Thank you, Beckford."

There was no reason to put off the inevitable. He'd been summoned, after all. Years of enduring his uncle's verbal abuse seemed to strip him of his confidence. Anywhere else, he stood proud, yet coming here always made him feel like a child. He would never reveal that his uncle had this power over him, but he loathed it all the same.

Upstairs, he stepped through the open archway that led to his uncle's sitting room. The man himself sat behind a desk, adding his signature and seal to a stack of documents.

The Earl of Marlbrook looked up and instantly sneered. "There's my pitiful excuse for an heir. Punctuality is the only credit to your character. Although I would have expected you to call earlier, considering the news you likely heard of my collapse."

"Of course," Griffin said quickly. He could hardly confess to having been avoiding him, could he? "I meant to call sooner but thought you were in need of rest."

His uncle scoffed. "*You thought?* Now there's a tale if ever there was one. If you had a thought in that pea-sized brain, it would never make past that crippled tongue of yours."

Griffin gritted his teeth. He knew that whatever he said would only be criticized, so he kept quiet. The sooner this exchange was over, the better.

"Eh?" The earl put his hand to his ear and then made a gesture of dismissal. "Bah! Just as I thought. Pitiful." He went back to signing papers. "Regardless, there's no getting around it now—you are my heir. I've instructed my man to take care of my affairs while I leave for my country estate. However, I don't intend to pay him a sum to travel back and forth, so I expect you to bring a full report at month's end. Can you manage that?"

"Yes, Uncle." As always, Griffin knew it was better to simply agree.

"Lord Coburn tells me you've yet to inquire about his stables." Without looking up, he dipped the quill into the inkpot and waggled a scolding finger in the same motion. "Because you didn't heed my advice, he's already sold the best of his stock."

"By then I'd already begun discussing a purchase with Lord Amberdeen." The prestigious mention earned Griffin a speculative glance and then a huff of indignation before Marlbrook set a new stack of documents before him.

"Then there's the matter of my late son's estate in Scotland, near Dumfries," his uncle continued, writing faster, the tip of the quill all but ripping through the parchment. "It will have to be managed, or let out, if you have no intention of living there."

"I will see to it, Uncle."

"I doubt you'll need such a residence, since you're incapable of ensnaring a bride," the earl snickered. "Even the ugly ones have their standards."

Not incapable but selective, Griffin thought, holding his tongue. There were dozens of young women who'd shown an interest. Though in truth, there was only one who kept him at odds with himself. Only one who'd made him alter his plans numerous times during the week. Only one who compelled him to drive down Danbury Lane half a dozen times each day.

In fact, as soon as he left here, he would do so again.

Delaney rushed out of number 27 Danbury Lane, clenching a missive between her teeth, while attempting to stuff Tillie's needlework into her reticule. She was going to be late. Again.

With only days before the wedding, this would be the last needlework circle with the four of them until Emma returned as a married woman.

Married, she thought with a pang of envy. A true marriage. She wondered if Emma would glow the same way Penelope did.

"Ow!" The needle jabbed her. Her brief bout of mawkishness evaporated as quickly as it had settled over her. The letter fell, unheeded, as she hastily stuck the tip of her finger into her mouth. *Blasted occupation*. She couldn't understand why her friends enjoyed it. She'd much rather go on outings or hold their meetings in the park.

"You seem to be in a hurry this afternoon, Miss McFarland," Griffin Croft said, startling her with his sudden appearance on the street in front of her.

Her heart pounded heavily. Somehow, she managed to convince herself that the reaction was from shock alone, even as her gaze roamed over him. It was impossible not to admire the way that man sat a horse. Or the way that his gray stallion complemented his gleaming black boots, slate coat, and top hat. Fittingly, he wore a horse collar knot in his cravat today.

As he dismounted, she watched the muscles of his thighs bunch and flex. The day grew suddenly warm. Too warm. Her spencer felt far too thick and constricting. "Is there a point of going anywhere if you are not in a hurry, Mr. Croft?"

He drew in an unmistakable *hiss* through his teeth in that instant, as if he'd landed wrong on his foot. It took him a moment before he turned to face her. But when he did, his eyes were that simmering lake water again. "There are some who prefer..."—his gaze dipped to her mouth—"a slower journey."

Yes, it was far too warm for a jacket today, she decided.

Delaney thought it best not to reply and focused on locating her fallen letter. While there'd been no return address when she saw it on the salver a moment earlier, she'd recognized the black seal as Montwood's. At last, after two weeks, he'd returned to town. Perhaps now they could settle matters before she changed her mind.

Changed her mind? Now, where had that thought come from, she wondered.

Unfortunately, her mental hesitation caused her not to notice that Griffin Croft had bent to retrieve her letter. She couldn't have him noticing the seal. It would only give him a reason to offer another unwanted opinion. The last thing she wanted was a lecture.

She reached out to snatch the letter. At the same time, the dratted needlework unfolded itself and slipped free, falling toward the gutter. "*Blast!* If I've ruined another pillow front then Tillie will..." Her words trailed off when she realized what she was saying. Or *admitting*, rather.

Mr. Croft came to her rescue, seizing the bundle before it touched the filth. He made a move to hand over both the letter and the fabric but at the last moment pulled them back. "Who's Tillie?"

"My maid," she huffed. "Now, kindly stop holding my needlework for ransom."

Again, he offered but withdrew, a grin toying with his mouth. "Why would your maid care if your needlework were ruined?"

She swallowed, hating the way his gaze sharpened on her as if she were a stain on a new gown. "She wouldn't."

"You pay your maid to do your needlework, don't you?" He issued a low, knowing chuckle. "And here I thought you couldn't surprise me more. Then again, I don't think I could imagine you sitting still and patiently plying your needle either."

He was too perceptive by half.

"Don't say anything, please," she said in a panic, feeling her shoulders tense as she glanced down the lane toward the Weatherstones' townhouse. "They mustn't find out. If they did..." She didn't want to put her fears into words. It could end her involvement in the circle if they discovered the truth. Losing the only friends she'd ever had would be too much to bear.

He stepped forward, concern etched in his expression. "Hold on, now. I was only teasing, Delaney—*Miss McFarland*," he corrected. But it still didn't change the fact that he'd spoken her name and with more tenderness than she could have imagined.

An odd current seemed to pass between them. Her breath caught in her throat. She hadn't been conscious of the strange connection they shared for several days. Not since that day she'd taken Griffin Croft to Warthall Place. Since that time, she'd done an excellent job of avoiding him. *Too excellent.* Though she didn't want to admit it, she feared that he no longer cared to annoy her. No longer cared to arrive at events she knew were outside of his schedule.

And yet, now he was on the street in front of her house, handing over her needlework. Was this meeting mere happenstance? She felt almost desperate to know. "Do you often ride down Danbury Lane?"

"Not often." Why he gave a wry smile, she couldn't guess. "This horse will be up for auction next week and the owner has allowed me to...sample the wares."

And he chose to ride down her lane, of all places?

Still, he hadn't answered her question. She dug a little deeper. "I imagine your sisters keep you quite busy."

"Somewhat," he said, but in a way that suggested he wished to be busier. "Though speaking of my sisters, they noticed your absence from Almack's the other night."

His sisters had noticed her absence, but he hadn't. Surely he'd been with them. Now, she almost wished she hadn't asked. "The reason should be obvious," she said quietly. Though it seemed he was waiting for an explanation. "I do not have a voucher."

If he noticed her embarrassment, he didn't reveal it. "I see. Then you must have attended..."

"Lord and Lady Finch hosted a ball." Quite possibly, it had been the dullest gathering in all of society. *Ball* was a very loose term, considering their only source of music was their daughter on the piano. "The gathering was likely smaller than at Almack's."

"Yes, I went there as well, but I did not arrive until later." His gaze dipped to her mouth with the same intensity she remembered from the Dorsets' conservatory. "I did not see you."

He'd gone to the Finches' ball as well? So then he'd attended Almack's and then Lord and Lady Finches'. Had he gone for the purpose of seeing her? Delaney could hardly breathe for thinking about it, and hoped—*prayed*—she wasn't grinning from ear to ear. "I left early."

He nodded, giving nothing away. "That explains it."

So he'd looked for her there. And today, it mattered enough to him to ask her about where she'd been. "Did you go to the Finches' for the purpose of—"

"I'm keeping you from your needlework—"

They spoke at the same time. She wondered if he would acknowledge having heard the first part of her question. He looked at her now as if he *had* heard. As if some part of him wanted to answer.

He searched her gaze. She waited. Surely he could guess what she'd been about to ask. Yet when a moment passed and he said nothing, she realized she'd let her imagination run away with her.

What a ninny! Hadn't she warned herself a thousand times against believing for a single moment that a man could form any romantic interest in her? And here she was, practically pining for Griffin Croft.

Without another word, he mounted his horse in one fluid motion, leaving her slightly dazzled. Ninny or not, she quite enjoyed the way he sat a horse.

"You have my letter," she said, looking up from his well-muscled thighs.

As if an afterthought, he handed down her note but not before he examined the seal on the back. A muscle ticked along the firm line of his jaw. "I see you've not abandoned your folly."

She lifted her hand and attempted to pull the envelope free, but he held it firmly. Her ire ignited. She yanked the letter free. Why could he never leave his opinions to himself? Out of everyone she knew, she thought he understood her reasoning. "I'm shocked you could still say such a thing after visiting Warthall Place. My own folly appears to be in underestimating you, Mr. Croft."

He matched her hard glare with one of his own. "The only person you've underestimated all along is yourself, Miss McFarland."

Then, with a snap of the reins, he left her standing there on the sidewalk, trying to figure out what he meant. Or why he pretended to care at all.

Frustrated, she ripped open the missive and read it.

At last! She let out a breath. Montwood wanted to meet. In the note, he gave instructions for the time and place in the park on the day following Emma's wedding. Yet at the very bottom, he'd written, "I beg of you, do not come alone."

What was it with men, believing they could order her around and dictate the course of her life? Frankly, she'd had enough.

If there was one thing Montwood needed to understand from the very beginning, it was that Delaney McFarland followed her own rules.

CHAPTER TWELVE

On the day following Emma and Rathburn's wedding, Delaney sat inside a closed carriage in the park, just as Montwood's note had instructed. Yesterday had been perfect for a wedding. Bright, golden sunlight filled the church. Emma looked positively stunning and so very regal in her gown. Rathburn had appeared a trifle panicked at first, but the moment Emma was standing by his side, an expression of utter awe fell over him.

It was that look that had drawn Delaney's first tear of the day.

The second had come at the lavish wedding breakfast. Facing the room at their table, Rathburn bent to whisper in Emma's ear frequently. And her friend blushed just as often. Delaney caught herself smiling at the memory, if a bit wistfully.

Then again, didn't every young woman dream of finding her perfect match? For Delaney, that dream would never be realized. Nonetheless, she would settle for having her other dreams realized. By marrying Montwood, she would have the freedom she desired, in addition to the funds with which to aid Mr. Harrison. That was all she needed.

Peering out through the curtains, she noticed a bank of trees up ahead and called to the driver. "Stop here, Dorsey." It was early, and the fashionable elite had yet to flood the grounds. She imagined that Montwood preferred clandestine meetings. Perhaps that would all change once they were married. Surely a sizable fortune would bring a charming, shadow-dweller like Montwood into the light.

No sooner had the horses stilled than the carriage door opened.

Montwood's dark head appeared, a dashing smile at the ready. "Miss McFarland, you are ever punctual." The comment proved how little they knew each other. Then, without invitation, he stepped inside and sat across from her.

Before he could pull the door closed, Buckley appeared outside. Beneath a halo of pale curls, he frowned and cast a somewhat murderous look toward Montwood. "Miss?"

Had he a gleaming sword and armor breastplate, Buckley could not have looked more like a knight determined to rescue her from ne'er-do-wells. "Everything is as it should be, Mr. Simms," she said fondly, fighting the urge to ruffle those curls.

He gave a curt nod, still casting daggers at Montwood and grudgingly closed the carriage door.

Across from her, Montwood pulled a frown as well. "He's quite fierce, isn't he? Though not much by way of a deterrent."

Puzzled more than alarmed, she asked, "What do you mean?"

"Only that if I chose to run off with you right now, there would be no one to stop me."

"**M**r. Croft, sir!"

At Tattersalls, Griffin turned toward the sound of the familiar voice and away from the crowd admiring his new horse, a beautiful gray high-stepper. "If it isn't young Mr. Simms. Tell me, what brings you here? If you are seeking my itinerary for the week, I shan't give it to you."

"It's Miss…McFarland…sir," the boy wheezed, out of breath.

Griffin quickly looked over his shoulder and pulled Buckley aside, away from the enclosure, so their exchange wouldn't be overheard. Fortunately, a new auction had begun and the noise of it gave him more privacy. "What is it?"

"She met a gentleman in the park just now. She didn't say his name, but I've seen him before and know him as Lord Lucan Montwood."

So, she'd met with him after all. Griffin's blood boiled instantly.

"It isn't just that," Buckley said, his mouth twisting into a frown, as if the name had soured on his tongue. "He said that if he should like to run off with her, there'd be no one to stop him."

Griffin stilled. Rage or not, panic sluiced through him. His heart stopped midbeat. "Where have they gone? Gretna Green?"

"No. No, sir." Buckley shook his head. "They're still across the way, by Deer Pond."

At this hour, there was no telling what clandestine activities could occur in the grove of trees that surrounded the water. He had no time to lose!

If I chose to run off with you right now, there would be no one to stop me.

A statement like that should've warranted a quiver of her pulse. A gasp. A shudder of dread. But all it did for Delaney was leave her feeling decidedly unmoved. "Not to worry. Dorsey's a crack shot with a whip."

Montwood offered an appraising grin. "I knew there was a reason I liked you. However, speaking of your driver…perhaps it would be best if the carriage were moving. Less suspicious, you see. And precisely why I begged you not to come alone."

Ignoring the warning in his tone, she called up to Dorsey and instantly felt the pull from the horses. But there was no pull to Montwood. No flutter in her stomach, no constricting of her lungs.

"I was afraid, after not seeing you or hearing from you for weeks, that you weren't considering the offer I made at the Dorset ball."

"I've done nothing but consider it," Montwood said quietly, as if more to himself than to her. "Day and night, that's all I've managed to think about."

She let out a breath, though she wasn't sure if it was a sigh of relief. "And you've come to a decision?"

He stared at her for a moment, his amber gaze searching her face as if for an answer. "First, I must tell you that you've honored me with your faith in my ability to uphold our bargain. Not many would trust me not to take advantage, contract or not, especially given the record of my past."

She assumed he was talking about his penchant for gambling…and losing. "I'm certain we both have instances in our pasts that have left us in the positions we're in today."

"Not like mine." He said the words with such dark finality that for the first time, she grew nervous. "While I cannot divulge the reason at the core of my failures, I will tell you that, if left another choice, I would never gamble another day in my life. But there are circumstances beyond my control that force me into the occupation." He looked at the shades covering the windows as if he could see through them to something far more disturbing than a view of the park. "Believe me, I've thought about every aspect your proposal, including how long it would take me to lose your fortune." He released an angry exhale that flared his nostrils. "Unfortunately, the answer is quite bleak."

A small laugh escaped her at the absurdity of the notion. "It would take two lifetimes to use such a sum."

He met her gaze and speared her with enough intensity that the laughter died on her lips. "Or a single year, in the hands of a desperate man."

Another current of nervousness raised the gooseflesh on her arms. She couldn't help but recall Mr. Croft's dire warning about putting herself under Montwood's control. "Are you desperate?"

"Yes. But not for any reason you could fathom. I made a mistake years ago. One that I will pay for until the end of my days, or the end of…" He shook his head, leaving his thought unfinished.

"Then you are here to tell me that you will not be accepting my proposal?" If he didn't marry her, she would be forced to start all over again with a new candidate.

"I cannot marry you," he said but leaned forward to take her hands. "I like you too much to bring you into my endless nightmare."

This was terrible news. So why did she feel a glimmer of relief? It wasn't as if she would marry for love. Yet, foolishly, her heart pined for it.

Montwood dropped her hands and straightened abruptly. Once again, he looked toward the curtains as if he could see through them. "I must take my leave now, and before we're discovered."

She listened for a moment to the sounds outside the carriage but heard nothing remarkable. Nothing other than horse hooves on the clay path, the jangle of rigging, and the music of songbirds off in the distance. What was it that caused his sudden alarm? "Do you know something I do not, Lord Montwood?" she asked, staring at him with curiosity.

"Perhaps. One such as I can never be too careful." He set his hand on the door and flashed one last charming smile before he slipped away.

Delaney lifted the curtain to see what might have alerted him, but she saw nothing. Not even Montwood's retreating figure. He'd simply disappeared. In fact, there wasn't anyone around this part of the park. Now that she thought about it, perhaps it was foolish to have met with him without a chaperone.

At least now it was over, and she didn't have to worry about Mr. Croft finding out.

She laughed to herself in relief before she called up to Dorsey. "I'm ready to return now." *With no one the wiser,* she thought with a grin.

"Beggin' your pardon, miss," her driver said. "Buckley ran off toward the corner and hasn't returned yet."

Why on earth would Buckley have gone to Hyde Park Corner? The only thing there was the tollbooth and…and Tattersalls. *No.*

She suddenly felt lightheaded. Mr. Croft had said something just the other day about acquiring a new horse. Surely Buckley wouldn't have gone in search of Griffin after Montwood entered carriage. It could be a coincidence…

She closed her eyes. No sooner had she put her hand to her head than she heard the approach of a horse. Then, too soon, she heard it stop. "Cor! That was so fast, I thought we were flying," Buckley exclaimed from outside the carriage.

We? Her heart dropped like a stone to the bottom of a well. She braced herself.

In the next instant, the door jerked open. Griffin Croft leapt inside as if prepared for battle. His face was etched in hard lines that likely would have intimidated Montwood if he'd still been there. As for her, she started and nearly let out a shriek but managed to hold it inside.

"What gives you the right to barge into this carriage?" Pleased with herself, she managed a believable bout of indignation.

Griffin Croft glared at her. "Do not test me, Miss McFarland. You were beyond foolish this morning, and after I'd specifically warned you to be on your guard."

His arrogance made her positively furious. "I am here in broad daylight in a public park, with a formidable driver who's a crack shot with a whip." Why she repeated this now, when it hadn't made a difference earlier, she didn't know. Still, she had a point to make. "Even you couldn't perceive my behavior as wholly reckless."

"Is that a challenge?"

She didn't bother to answer and instead crossed her arms over her chest, returning his glare. From the open carriage door, she saw Buckley holding the reins of the horse and watching their exchange with frank fascination.

Delaney was about to order Mr. Croft to leave at once, but then he reached over and closed the door. A wild glimmer darted across his lake-water irises. Her pulse crackled, and a heated shiver rushed through her. Was he going to kiss her again? Prove how dangerous it was to be alone with a desperate man? Strangely, the idea wasn't as unappealing as it ought to have been. Quite the opposite.

"This primitive display of yours has gone quite far enough," she said sternly. Or at least, she hoped it sounded as such. "You have certainly made your point. It terrifies me to think that right at this moment, I could be sitting across from someone who sent a request to meet him, in addition to a plea that I bring an escort." Hmm...it probably didn't suit her argument to add the last part. Blast her mouth for speaking too freely.

He moved to the edge of the seat across from hers, which forced her to lift her chin to look up at him. His nearness had a terrible effect on her equilibrium. Looking into his eyes just now, it felt as if she were tilting forward. "You are fortunate to have men looking out for your welfare instead of looking to take advantage. Am I to assume your arrangement with Montwood is settled?"

"In regard to me, you are to assume nothing, because you have no claim over me." The words came out with much less vehemence and more breathy excitement than intended. Delaney noted the change in his expression too, how the hardness slipped away as his gaze slipped to her mouth. She shook her head in a way that sent several curls loose. "I am cross with Buckley for having gone to you."

"Do not blame him. He was worried about you." Griffin Croft lifted a hand to smooth back those tendrils, his gloves lightly grazing her cheek. A tremor coursed through her.

"As sweet as that is," she said, fighting the urge to shake her head and send dozens more curls free, simply to feel his touch again, "I would rather he didn't run to you."

"Who else, then?" When it appeared as if her recalcitrant curls refused to heed his instruction, he released a slow breath as if frustrated, and lowered his hand. "Do you have another candidate lined up for your marriage bargain?"

"*Another?*" she asked in a whisper. "How do you know it isn't Montwood?"

He gave a slight shrug. "Your reaction told me as much. You'll find I know more about you than you believe."

Sitting this close to Griffin made her feel prickly and overly warm. "Surely, you have other things to occupy your time than to concern yourself with whom I marry. After all, it will not be you. Therefore, I don't see why you pretend to care."

It was only a whispered parry, but apparently it struck nerve. His irises grew dark and clouded. Though he didn't move, it seemed as if he'd crossed further into her space. "And why not?"

She stilled. "Why not...*what?*"

"Why wouldn't you choose to marry someone like me"—he said, seeming to draw even closer—"though not me, of course."

Not me, of course. He emphasized the words much the same as she had, as if the fact that they would never marry was a foregone conclusion. And yet for reasons she couldn't fathom, it irked her. Annoyance notwithstanding, she would never even consider marrying Griffin Croft *or* someone like him.

She stopped leaning forward and sat straighter. "I told you my reasons. I won't marry someone like you—or you, of course—because you require an heir. I want a marriage in name only. I want to live a life of my choosing."

"Yes, we've already established the reason for that. But you *could* marry a man who shared your vision of Warthall Place." He hesitated, searching her gaze. "Surely that would be something to consider."

Suddenly, she grew conscious of each breath. The air tasted stale in this carriage, as if no amount of wind could slip through the seams in the door. "No," she said, her voice a rasp. Lifting a hand to her throat, she unfastened the top button of her spencer. "I cannot breathe in here, Mr. Croft. Please let me go."

It didn't matter that he wasn't actually touching her—she felt restricted by him all the same.

"Are you ill?" He reached out as if to take her in his arms. Against all reason, she wanted him to. Instead, he fisted his hands and dropped them to his sides.

She tried to breathe, but no air filled her lungs. "I'm sure it's nothing. A bit of dust from the path perhaps. I am well."

"Then allow me to see you home."

She shook her head. "No. I can manage on my own. I will be just fine on my own."

That was the life she wanted for herself, after all.

Chapter Thirteen

"Who is she, Griff?"

At the sound of his mother's voice, Griffin turned from the window. Since night had fallen hours ago, there hadn't been much to look at anyway—only purplish shadows that looked haunted to him. The same way Miss McFarland's eyes had been that morning in the carriage over two weeks ago. Since then, he had not seen her. Or rather, he *had* seen her at Haversham's, but he had not spoken to her.

He lifted his brow, as if he hadn't any idea to what his mother was referring. "She?"

Octavia Croft's keen, dark eyes narrowed. She crossed the drawing room. "The same one who has put this"—her finger touched just above the bridge of his nose—"furrow between your brows. I've seen it more often than not in the past few weeks. If truth be told, I've even seen it since near the start of the Season."

"There is no one," he said, resigned. "Perhaps that is why I possess the mark of a worrier. I know you need me to find a bride. With little more than a month remaining of the Season, I've failed you yet again."

"There's still time," Calliope said from the doorway. Dressed in her night rail and dressing gown, she hid a yawn behind her hand. Then, as if to explain her appearance, when the others had gone to bed earlier, she said, "I couldn't sleep. I've decided to tell cousin Pamela that I cannot be her bridesmaid."

Thankfully, this took their mother's focus off him. She moved to Calliope's side and led her to the sofa. "I know you'd once had your heart set on Lord Brightwell for yourself. But my dear, you made your choice years ago. You must put this matter behind you. We are family, after all." She shook her head and released a sigh. "I'm grateful the two of you didn't end up engaged first like that poor Miss Wakefield. I feel just terrible for her, now shunned by most of society."

"At least she has the support of her friends. They did not abandon her. In fact, I believe the elder Miss McFarland is amongst them." Calliope looked across the room to Griffin as she burrowed into the corner of the sofa and hid another yawn. "And speaking of Miss McFarland...I could always take a lesson from her and schedule other plans for the day of the wedding."

"Now, what's this?" his mother asked as she settled a fringed shawl over his sister's lap. "I thought after our lovely visit early on, she was through with that nonsense, as if she could have helped what happened. I would hate to think of her staying away from any event for fear that being seen with you would cause that scandal to resurface." She asked. "After all, that is no way for a young woman to find a husband."

Griffin chuckled wryly. "I can assure you that Miss McFarland is quite fearless in that regard. She knows exactly what she wants in a husband." *And what she doesn't.*

Nevertheless, she was a mystery. Because, if he hadn't known better, some part of her had seemed terrified by the idea of marriage—at least, a marriage in the truest sense. She wanted a marriage in name only. So what was it then? Was she afraid of the marriage bed?

He dismissed the thought almost instantly. When they'd kissed, she'd shown no indication of fear or revulsion. In fact, her response had been as passionate and uninhibited as everything else about her.

"Fearless?" Calliope asked, her gaze far away. "I don't think any young woman can truly be fearless."

He thought of how Delaney had stood up for Buckley and how much she wanted to aid Mr. Harrison. "I think Miss McFarland is one of the bravest persons I've ever had the pleasure of knowing." At least, until he'd mentioned marriage.

"Then perhaps spending an afternoon with Miss McFarland might be the perfect solution for you, Calliope," their mother said as she dropped a few peppermint leaves into a waiting teacup. "We should invite her to Springwood House when you visit Pamela. After all, it's only a two-hour ride from London. Perfect for a single day's outing. She'll be just the distraction from any of your other worries."

Calliope mused over the possibility for what seemed like—at least to Griffin—an eternity. "I do enjoy her company. Though, I'm certain she won't attend if she knows Griffin will be with us."

"Your brother will spend most of his time at the earl's country estate, nearly five miles from my sister's house."

Both his mother and sister turned to him as if waiting for an objection. Griffin controlled his features, refusing to reveal any eagerness. After an absence apart, he was looking forward to seeing Delaney more than he cared to admit. Much more. "Do what you will. Though I doubt she will accept."

And yet, he sincerely hoped she would.

"What are you doing?" Bree asked from the doorway of Delaney's bedchamber.

Without looking up, Delaney stacked a tin of biscuits on top of a tin of chocolates and began to tie them with a ribbon. "I'm putting together a parcel to cheer Merribeth." She was devastated for her friend. Merribeth's romantic sensibilities had been crushed by the one man who should have cherished them. Instead, Mr. Clairmore merely gave her a reason to doubt the existence of true love.

"It was an abominable thing for her betrothed to do, breaking their five-year engagement to marry someone else." Bree ambled gracefully into the room. "Her story has been told again and again as a cautionary tale for us all to hold fast to our honor."

"Merribeth has her honor," Delaney snapped. Pulling too tightly on the ribbon, she crumpled it beyond repair. "The only one who has lost it, if he ever had any, is Mr. Clairmore."

Her sister paled. "I didn't mean to suggest..." She swallowed, the remaining words left unspoken. Ruination for any young woman was a terrible fate.

Delaney smoothed down her phoenix feathers when she realized Bree wasn't attacking her friend. She went to the carved rosewood chest of drawers by the window and retrieved a fresh ribbon.

"It actually made me wonder about Mother and Father," her sister said, staring at the miniatures of their parents on the far wall. "Is love such a fleeting thing, do you think?"

That exact question turned a constant wheel in Delaney's mind. "We have proof enough within these walls. Though I would hate to think it's true in all cases, especially since Emma and Rathburn have only been married a fortnight. They deserve a lifetime of happiness together."

Bree released sigh. "I wish Mother had taken me with her. Having a Season is not as fun as I'd always thought it would be. I live under constant fear of doing something wrong, of becoming—"

"An outcast like your sister?" Delaney supplied dryly.

"Hardly anyone mentions your scandal any longer. Since the Earl of Marlbrook retired to the country for his health, they are more concerned with Mr. Croft and discovering who he'll choose for a wife." She paused to bend down and smooth her hair in the vanity mirror, her gaze flitting to Delaney's. "Marlene Wickworth believes it will be her because he danced the waltz with her at Almack's."

Knowing she was being watched, Delaney returned her focus to tying the bow. "I hope they will be happy together."

"It is unlikely. When he saw her at the Porter ball a few nights later, he quickly introduced her to a gentleman standing beside him."

Delaney smirked, easily picturing him doing just that. The same way she'd foisted Elena Mallory on him. It was hard to believe that was a month ago now. So much had happened since then. So much had changed in her.

"Phoebe and Asteria have both mentioned that he's been distracted of late." Bree's statement earned a look up from the bundle. "They suspect he might have feelings for someone, but he's so reserved, they cannot be certain. He never appears to like one dance partner more than another."

It took Delaney a moment to realize she was simply staring at her sister, the tail ends of another ruined ribbon in her grasp. Her heart lurched backward, as if it had been pinched. Hard.

Had Griffin Croft chosen a bride? The thought pained her more than she cared to admit. *Why wouldn't you choose to marry someone like me…*

Little more than two weeks ago—for the most fleeting moment—she'd actually thought he might have considered asking her.

Though not me, of course.

In front of her sister, she dared not reveal her secret musings. Bree was too observant and far too eager to share her observations with others, namely Griffin's sisters. "Perhaps you are confusing arrogance for reservation on his part. He's likely scolding each one of his partners in his mind."

"That is something Phoebe and Asteria would say." Bree grinned. "Strange, but I didn't think you were very well acquainted with Mr. Croft."

Delaney knew the exact shade of his eyes, the texture of his lips, the flavor of his tongue, and the feel of his hands memorizing each of her vertebrae. She knew his character as well. And even though he arrogantly believed she should heed his advice without question, he'd still kept her secrets and never once used them against her. "Your assumption is correct. I hardly know him at all. It was just a passing observation." She shrugged and walked to the chest for another ribbon. "You know my tendency to speak before thinking."

"Are you unwell? Your cheeks are rather flushed."

"It must be from the sun coming in through the windows," she said before realizing it was raining at that very moment.

Fortunately, she was saved further inquiry when one of the latest maids knocked on her door. "Beg pardon, miss, but you've a caller. The young woman gave this to Hershwell." She stepped forward and handed Delaney the card.

Bree looked over her shoulder. "Calliope Croft? Imagine that. We were just speaking about her brother. Perhaps she's come to share a bit of news regarding his mystery woman."

Delaney's stomach felt queasy. "I don't think we've established he has a mystery woman."

"Well, there's only one way to find out."

Downstairs, they greeted Calliope Croft and summarily ordered refreshments as they settled amongst the soft cushions of the chairs and settee. In the first half hour, they chatted amiably about the rain's making way for new flowers and various topics of no consequence until they'd run them all dry.

"I imagine you're wondering why I'm here, Miss McFarland," Calliope said after a while. "That is to say, I would come to call without a purpose in mind. I've found our few brief encounters quite enjoyable. I think we could be friends."

"Of course. We are already friends," Delaney said and reached across the low table to squeeze Calliope's hand. "If you called for any purpose, it would be a delight. My sister knows well enough I could produce an hour's worth of conversation by discussing the latest ribbons at Haversham's."

Bree laughed. "Sadly, it is the truth. Without you here, I'm certain we would both be at that particular shop, replenishing her supply."

"I must admit, I'm rather fond of Haversham's as well. You were not too boastful in your praise." Calliope smiled. "I wish we could have visited with you when we saw you there the other day. Although, I'm hoping to talk my brother into escorting us again someday soon."

"Nonsense. We could go together. No need for your brother's escort," Delaney added, in case it sounded as if she wanted Griffin to escort her or to call on her. She hoped her expression didn't give away the fact that she *had* wondered what it would be like if he did. "Besides, I'm certain he has more important matters to attend."

The fact that he'd been escorting his sisters *and* Elena Mallory had brought her no end of irritation. At least, she told herself, it was *irritation* and not something more detrimental to her heart, such as jealousy. Whatever the feeling had been, it had raged inside her for the past two days.

"Especially now when rumor suggests he's decided on a bride," Bree added, but with a peculiar intensity, as if she were informing Calliope instead of asking her to prove the rumor.

Delaney wondered if her sister was capable of subterfuge. By now, she should know it was always better to draw out the information by pretending disinterest. For that reason, and most assuredly not out of her own curiosity, Delaney said, "I'm certain he's received ample encouragement from a select few."

There now—that was a perfect example. She hoped her sister would take the lesson.

Calliope pulled her gaze from Bree and blinked at Delaney. "Yes. It is my understanding that he has someone in mind. So far, she's been the only one he's favored all Season."

"Oh?" Delaney swallowed. There it was again, that painful pinching sensation. She'd hoped Calliope would admit that there wasn't anyone to whom Griffin paid enough attention to warrant the rumor.

"It can't be true," Bree said on a gasp. "Our cousin Elena Mallory had said almost those exact words."

Delaney stared wide-eyed at her sister, even as a terrible sickness began roiling in her stomach. *Not her.* Anyone else but her. And yet…no. Not anyone else either. *It should be me,* a fearsome voice whispered in her mind, startling her. If she didn't know herself better, she'd almost believe this was jealousy. She'd almost believe that…she was falling in love in with Griffin Croft.

Delaney fought the urge to lower her head in shame. After all the careful planning to live a life of her own choosing, had she ruined it all by repeating her mother's mistake?

Blast it all!

"It would be unfair of me to divulge a name until he's made his intentions known to the young woman herself." Calliope shifted in her seat. "And while we are on the topic of weddings, I wondered if I might ask a favor."

"Of course," Delaney said, employing her most practiced smile in an effort not to reveal her inner distress. "You need only ask."

"You are too kind, but I am not above taking advantage in this particular instance," Calliope said with a small laugh. "You see, my cousin is about to marry a man whom I once considered a possibility for my own future."

"Oh dear! What happened?" Bree asked with an embarrassing lack of tact.

"You don't have to say anything," Delaney added quickly, casting a look of reproach to her sister.

"It's all right. After all, I believe you deserve to know why I would ask this favor of you," Calliope began. "It happened at the end of my first Season when I was perhaps too young to know better. Lord Brightwell had asked for permission to court me, and my father had given his consent. It seemed our betrothal would happen any day. When the happy event occurred, however, I did not accept Lord Brightwell's proposal." She looked across the table with such regret that it silenced any impending question from Bree. "Because he is now marrying my cousin, I should like your company when I visit her in two weeks' time."

Delaney knew what this meant. If she accepted this invitation, she would be linking her name with the Crofts, possibly opening herself up to scandal. Strangely, she no longer cared if their names were linked in scandal or otherwise. Perhaps she felt this way because she knew Mr. Croft was about to make a declaration of love for another woman.

She refused to believe it was because of a foolish yearning on her part.

Chapter Fourteen

Griffin entered his uncle's grand estate with none of the dread he'd felt weeks ago. In fact, after having ridden out of town on his horse alongside the carriages with his mother, sisters, and the Misses McFarland inside, he felt peculiarly invigorated by this jaunt in the country.

The fact that Miss McFarland had accepted his sister's invitation said a great deal. A month ago, she was still avoiding him at every turn, hoping their names would never be linked again. But now…it appeared she didn't mind at all.

"Good morning, Uncle," he said as the butler led him into the east wing breakfast room of the Marlbrook estate. The room hosted a rectangular table, situated as a grand desk would be, with a single chair facing away from the window, affording his great-uncle a view of the entire room. Without a word, the Earl of Marlbrook made it perfectly clear that no one was invited to join him.

The older man squinted and gave a sniff of disapproval before he returned to his egg cup. "And here is my bacon-brained heir, coming to pay a call. I hardly recognized you without your tongue tied around your teeth. Then again, you've only spoken three words. There's still plenty of time."

Griffin stood in front of the intractably unforgiving Earl of Marlbrook and for the first time in his life, he did not cower inwardly. Now, he stood tall. Inside and out.

He recalled the day Miss McFarland had faced that clerk and dared challenge him. Even if the man had been a duke, he did not doubt that her response would have been the same. "I am not a child anymore, Uncle. Your insults only make me pity the man who'd always waited until no one was around to overhear him tormenting a boy for a speech impediment."

It would have been just as cowardly to taunt a boy like Buckley for his missing arm.

As a child, Griffin had been taught to revere his elders and hadn't once questioned his mistreatment. In fact, he never told his parents, because he'd been brought so low by his great-uncle that he feared they would also see him as a disappointment.

It was strange to imagine he'd ever felt that way. In this moment, it was as if his eyes were finally open. A change had come over him in recent weeks. It had been so gradual that he'd hardly noticed it. Yet now, he actually felt it stirring inside him.

Fearlessness.

It was bound to happen, he supposed. After all, he'd had an excellent tutor in Delaney McFarland. He credited the beginning of this change to the moment she'd shared with him her hopes for Warthall Place. However, he suspected it had started much sooner. Because of her, he felt strong enough to stand up to the great-uncle who'd been a vicious bully to him whenever they'd been alone together.

"Pity, you say?" He scoffed, and a bit of masticated egg flew onto the table. "You who cannot find a wife willing to accept you for fear of crippled offspring."

The insult made it no farther than the bit of egg. In fact, Griffin laughed. "Your condescension has no effect on me. I have been liberated beyond your reach and no longer care for your opinion, good or otherwise."

"How d-dare you s-speak to me in s-such a—" The earl's words died suddenly. At the sound of his own stammering, his face went ghostly white.

"Do not worry, Uncle. You will receive no abuse from me. Perhaps I'll even hire a nurse to take care of you until your…*ailment* subsides," Griffin said with a satisfied grin. Without permission, he approached the table and laid the reports he'd brought down on the corner. "And make no mistake," he added with utter certainty before he quit the room. "*I* am the selective one, and I'll choose the wife best suited to me, not one who must live up to your impossible standards."

And he had the perfect candidate in mind.

"Forgive me for beaming so, Miss McFarland," Phoebe Croft said as their small group walked the lovely grounds at Springwood House. "I'm still in a state of shock that you chose to join us today."

"But it's a very pleased state of shock," Asteria added.

"I don't know why," Bree said with her own grin, as if she shared a confidence with the twins. "After all, it wasn't your brother who asked. He's the only person she avoids."

Delaney gave her sister a hard look. She didn't want anyone to make too much of her acceptance of Calliope's invitation. Regardless, she wouldn't insult them either by telling them the reason was because she had no prior engagements. Besides, even she knew it was more than that. Agreeing to accompany his sisters was the closest she'd come to acknowledging her emerging feelings for Griffin Croft.

Emerging feelings? She couldn't lie to herself. The way she felt for him had already surfaced. Only…she was too afraid to admit them aloud.

"True. By accepting our invitation, however, your sister is demonstrating a great deal of bravery," Calliope said, tucking a book of sonnets into a pocket sewn into her blue striped day dress.

"I wouldn't call it bravery." Delaney gave a self-derisive laugh. "It isn't as if you're a fearsome lot."

"Oh, but it's true," Calliope said with sincere nod. "Griffin said himself that you were one of the bravest people he's had the pleasure of knowing."

Delaney might have stumbled if not for Phoebe's steady arm linked with hers. "He said that about me?"

"Does that surprise you?" Asteria skipped ahead and turned around to face the group as she walked backward. "I don't see why it would."

"Well…" She hoped the sudden rush of elation didn't show on her face. "He hardly knows me."

"That isn't true," Bree added. "He's known you since your debut and that was nearly fifteen months ago. Paulette Hornsby had only known Mr. Lassiter for three days before they were betrothed."

"Who said anything about betrothal?" Delaney stopped in her tracks, her breath coming up short. She looked to her sister and to each of the Croft women in order to make her point. "Please do not imagine I have any designs or inclinations where Mr. Croft is concerned."

"Of course not," Calliope said in a rush. Out of the corner of her eye, Delaney saw Phoebe give Bree's sleeve a tweak. "I'm sure your sister was merely making an observation. We are all friends, are we not?"

"We can certainly have a pleasant visit away from the pressure of the Season," Asteria added. "I say we spend the rest of the time talking about the matches that have been made thus far. Phoebe and I have a list. It used to be Calliope's, but we've added to it."

"A list?" That sparked Delaney's interest.

"Oh yes, complete with names of all ne'er-do-wells, rakes, and—"

"Fortune hunters?"

Beside her, Phoebe frowned. "Now, that I think on it, I believe we left the list at home. Didn't we, Asteria?"

Her sister nodded. A look of some mysterious understanding passed between them. "Then perhaps we can all walk to the Gingerbread Cottage."

"A gingerbread cottage! What fun," Bree said with a clap.

Calliope smiled. "It isn't really made of gingerbread, of course. When Griffin and I were little, we used to sneak gingerbread out of our aunt's house and eat it in secret. Over time, when the twins discovered us—and even more recently, with Tess—the small cottage on the property became known as the Gingerbread Cottage."

"It's a very snug structure but tall," Phoebe said. "I think we can all crowd inside. Would you like to see it?"

Delaney nodded. "I'm too curious by half not to see it. It's a shame we don't have a few pieces of your cook's delicious gingerbread to enjoy."

She waited for one of them to make a reference to it being Griffin's favorite as well. Thankfully, no one did.

"That is a wonderful idea. Perhaps our aunt has some gingerbread or biscuits for us," Phoebe said. "Asteria and I will hurry back to the house to check and meet you there."

Calliope looked up at the sky. "You'd best make haste, for I believe Mother was right. It does look like rain."

The twins were off in a flash of pastel pink and yellow.

"I hope Mother doesn't catch them holding their skirts so high," Calliope added with a laugh before she turned and pointed further down the path. "The cottage is just up ahead and around that thicket of trees."

It was a quaint little wood on the Springwood lands, and Delaney found herself immensely glad to have accepted the invitation. Yet she had to admit that she was disappointed— in a very small degree, of course—that her path hadn't crossed with Mr. Croft's, other than from the view through the carriage window. In fact, she'd hoped for an accidental sighting of those lake-water eyes.

And just as the thought of water entered her thoughts, a single fat raindrop fell on her nose. She looked up. Yes, it did indeed look like rain.

Bree gasped and wiped a drop from her cheek. "I didn't dress for the rain, and these are new slippers."

Delaney hadn't expected rain either. Being too warm, she'd left her spencer and hat in the house. "It is only a spring rain, more likely to diminish before you'd make it back to the house."

"True," Calliope said.

Bree shook her head and stared at Griffin's sister with the strangest intensity. "I want to go back to the house, but I would feel strange returning without a member of the family with me. Surely, Delaney could go on alone and wait for…*us*. You said yourself that the cottage is just up ahead. And then, after the rain has stopped, we may all gather for a celebration of sorts."

A celebration picnic? Delaney wondered what Bree could possibly want to celebrate here at Springwood House with the Croft sisters. But before she could inquire, Calliope spoke.

"That is the perfect idea. More perfect than even I could have planned." A slow smile spread over Calliope's face as if a taper had suddenly been lit inside her. She reached forward and squeezed Bree's hand before she faced Delaney. "We will join you right after the rain stops. And please, make yourself comfortable. Our aunt usually keeps a blanket and a small stack of wood inside."

Delaney felt her brow pucker as the exchange grew stranger by the moment. "If what you say is true, then we are all closer to the cottage than to the house. Surely if we—"

Calliope interrupted her and took a step backward in the direction of the house. "This is Pamela's shawl. If I return it wet, I'll never hear the end of it."

"We must hurry!" Bree said with a bright grin on her face as well.

Very peculiar. And somewhat suspicious. Yet Delaney was too curious to see the cottage, where Griffin had played as a child, to argue.

Then, no sooner had they set off in opposite directions than a sudden gust blew through the trees. Looking up at the sky, Delaney noticed that it had darkened considerably. Perhaps this wasn't going to be a typical spring rain after all.

She had her answer within the next thirty steps. Her green muslin was no match for the swirling wind or the heavy drops that started to fall. By the time she reached the small stone cottage, nestled in a thicket of birch trees, she was quite thoroughly drenched.

Five miles down the road from his uncle's, Griffin stopped cold beneath the arched entry to his aunt's house. "You left her out in this?"

Calliope had rushed to open the door the instant he'd jumped off his horse. Now, she was standing just inside the foyer, with worry in her pleading gaze. "We never expected a storm. It was only supposed to be a short spring rain.

And besides, she isn't *out* in it. I assume she made it the cottage."

"You *assume!*" Now worry lanced through him. A river of water poured from the brim of his hat. It was pointless to waste another moment talking to his sister. "I'm going after her."

CHAPTER FIFTEEN

Nestled securely in the thicket of trees, the tiny cottage had managed to stay quite dry. Delaney, however, had not. When she'd first arrived, she was dripping from head to foot all over the hard-packed clay floor.

Calliope had been right on several accounts. The cottage was quite snug and clean as well. A single chair—sturdy but old and flecked with aged red paint—stood by a crescent-shaped fireplace recessed into the stone wall. A basket of firewood and kindling lay at the hearth with a cloth-wrapped bundle of tinder and flint. And a fringed blanket was draped over a peg on the wall.

As the spring rain turned into a storm outside, Delaney made herself more comfortable and started a fire. Yet even then, she couldn't remove the chill that covered her from head to toe. Her clothes were still dripping wet. She couldn't very well stand before the fire, expecting her clothes to dry quickly. They needed to be wrung out.

Shivering, she looked outside to the raging storm. Surely neither Bree nor Calliope would venture out in this. And who knew how long the storm would last? Delaney wasn't about stand there with her teeth chattering the whole time. She stripped out of her dress, petticoat, shoes, and stockings, leaving her clad in only her somewhat dry chemise. She hoped that by the time the rain stopped, her clothes would be dry. To make sure of it, she retrieved a few fallen branches from outside the door, hung her clothes across them, and positioned each by the fire to dry.

When that was all settled, she took the blanket off the peg, gave it a good shake out the door, and then wrapped it around her body, tossing one end over her shoulder and fashioning it like a tartan.

Immensely pleased with her ingenuity, Delaney laughed and spun in a circle. "Anyone who ever doubted my ability to manage the rest of my life on my own should see me now."

A rumble of thunder answered, causing another shiver to race through her. Moving across the room, she opened the narrow door to appraise the storm. That was the moment, she realized, that it was not thunder she'd heard after all. It was a horse and rider.

And none other than Griffin Croft.

Delaney's heart raced. What was he doing here? He couldn't find her. Not like this.

She shrank back from the door, her hand holding the blanket in place. She was suddenly very aware of how it only draped to her knees and left one shoulder exposed, revealing the strap of her chemise.

In a panic, she looked around the room. There had to be something she could use to make herself more presentable or to hide her altogether. And yet, there was nothing. Her clothes were still drying. Even if they weren't wet, she didn't have time to don so much as her petticoat.

His horse stopped directly in front of the cottage, and he leapt down in a rush. Water sluiced from his hat and clothes as he hastily tied the reins around a low-hanging branch.

Frozen in dread, all she could do was stand there and watch as he turned and saw her.

The moment he glimpsed Delaney McFarland's bare feet, Griffin halted midstride. Slowly, his gaze traveled up over her slender ankles and shapely calves, to the edge of the russet blanket. He should have looked away, but he simply couldn't. Greedily, perhaps foolishly, he continued to drink in the sight past the curve of her hips and to that delectably small bosom swathed in a gather of fabric that draped temptingly over one shoulder. Her other shoulder was all but nude, dressed only in a scrap of transparent silk that matched the creamy skin bared to him. Lightning swift arousal tore through him, thickening his blood and making his heart pound hard, laboring for every beat.

Those pink lips formed a round O of astonishment. Her untamable hair framed her face. A few dark curling tendrils stuck to her cheeks and neck, revealing their wetness.

Coming to his senses, he took a step forward to get out of the rain.

However, he hadn't enough sense to duck his head and collided with the stone frame of the door, hard enough that he heard the thud of his forehead cracking against it. He staggered back a step. In fact, he might have fallen if not for Delaney's sudden grip on his waistcoat.

She released him the moment he righted himself. "Why are you here?" she asked.

"I should think the answer obvious." Then again… considering the circumstances, perhaps it wasn't completely apparent. She might wonder if he had other designs. He would ease her mind on that account—at least for the time being. Now was certainly not the time to profess his intentions. "Calliope told me you were here. Alone. In the storm."

"Well, you needn't have come." She bristled and moved backward into the cottage. In four steps she was already to the far end, where she positioned herself behind a lone chair.

"Needn't have come?" Overwhelming worry had driven him here in the first place. And all she could say was that he needn't have come? "I would be dry and enjoying a nice brandy right now, if not for you."

He was to the chair in two strides. The sounds of water dripping from his coat and the crackling of the small fire echoed around them. Removing his gaze from her for the first time, he noted the snugness of the space. Although perhaps it seemed even smaller because her clothes were hanging on branches to dry.

He stared at her dress and petticoat, both transparent from the rain. He should leave. Now. He should return to the house before…

Seeing her cross her arms beneath that tantalizing bosom of hers, he forgot what he was thinking.

For months, Griffin had been crazed by desire for this woman. There was no hope for it. He'd tried to fight his attraction for her, but the bristly and impulsive Delaney McFarland was a constant temptation. "You seem to have made yourself at home."

"Would you have me sit here in dripping clothes until I caught a cold while waiting for the storm to end?"

"No. You have the right of it." No other woman could deliver a set-down while dressed in a mere blanket and make it sound so convincing. "I should like to remove my coat as well, but the only way would be to peel it off like a banana skin."

She glanced down to the puddle forming at his feet. "You could catch cold," she said softly. Was that concern in her voice?

Catch cold? He nearly laughed. At the moment, he felt like he was on fire. "Not likely."

Then, without hesitation, she moved behind him. "I cannot stand by and allow your arrogance to be the death of you."

If an argument had been on his lips, it was soon reduced to ashes when he felt her hands on his shoulders and the way they slid to his collar. He shuddered. Arrogance wouldn't be the death of him, but she might.

Determined to remain in control and not reveal how much she affected him, he pushed apart the lapels and shrugged. It loosened enough for her to take a firmer grip. She yanked, but the coat seemed fused to the thick muscles of his upper arms. He'd ridden hard, so it was no wonder the coat was tighter than usual.

"How did you manage to don this coat in the first place?" she asked with grunt, jerking the fabric down another inch.

He glanced back and saw her struggling to keep the end of the blanket in place. Another heady rush of arousal filled him. He looked forward quickly but let his head fall back on an oath. "It wasn't wet when I dressed this morning. Perhaps it has shrunk." His coat was the *only* thing growing smaller on him at the moment.

"Or perhaps your shoulders are too…large," she said, her voice as insubstantial as that strap across her bare skin. He felt the barest brush of her fingers over his shoulders. "D-did you get this way from boxing?"

"Amongst other things." He'd employed many strenuous activities of late to keep thoughts of her from distracting him. Tempting him.

"Mr. Harrison told me that you went to see the boys and offered them boxing lessons."

He gave a sound of assent but made no comment. He hadn't been able to get Delaney or Warthall Place off his mind and had decided to offer his own brand of support.

In the next few moments, with their efforts combined, the jacket slid off and fell to the floor with a soggy *plop*. Keeping his gaze averted—or trying to—he picked up the coat, took it over to the door, and wrung it out. By the time he stepped in front of the fire, she'd moved her garments out of the way to make a place for his.

"Now, sit down and let me take a look at that bump," she ordered, as if expecting no argument.

He was about to tell her that he'd received greater blows from Everhart than that little bump from the door, but instead, he found himself obeying.

"Close your eyes…please."

When he did, she stepped in front of him.

The edge of the blanket brushed his legs, just above the knee. The touch was light, almost imperceptible, and yet he felt it within the marrow of his bones. Unable to help himself, he opened his eyes to slits and watched her movements. Her soft hands brushed his hair back, and her fingers tenderly prodded the flesh above his brow.

"Do you think I will live?" He wasn't certain he would at the moment, not when every drop of his blood rushed to fill his erection. There was no concealing it in his current position either. The thick ridge was outlined clearly beneath his damp breeches.

"I've no doubt your head is hard enough to withstand numerous collisions," she teased.

Then, as she took a step back, the end of the blanket fell free of her shoulder, exposing her. The small bosom he'd fantasized about for months flashed before him. Her transparent chemise did nothing to block his view of the delicate teardrop-shaped swells or the pale pink nipples near the center.

Automatically, she went to cover herself, and in the same instant, untamable desire claimed him, taking control. He caught her hands. "Don't. Please let me…just this once."

Restraint abandoned him. He couldn't take it. He had to touch her, taste her, feed this growing need within him. Perhaps it was the bump on his head that had addled his brain, but he could no longer control his actions.

Drawing her hands behind her back, he left her open and exposed for him. "You're perfect. Just as I've imagined. Better than each of my fantasies."

She didn't resist, but let him trail a finger along the outer edge of one breast and then the other. "You've imagined this? With me?" Her voice came out on a breath, as if awed by his admission.

"Countless times." And yet the color of her flesh was a surprise. Her breasts were white and flawless as porcelain. The puckered center was a delicate pink hue, paler even than the blush of her cheeks. They appeared almost fragile, or perhaps like pink-tipped meringues that would dissolve on his tongue.

He tugged her forward and closed his mouth over one peak. She let out a muffled cry. The silk rasped against his tongue, but still he could feel her ruched flesh beneath. It wasn't enough. He needed to taste the rain on her skin.

Griffin released her hands in order to lower the straps. Slowly, he pulled the insubstantial fabric down, inch by inch, below her breasts and to her slender waist. Setting his hands on her skin, he explored the softness of her stomach, the slender cage of her ribs, and finally those perfect mounds.

He feasted on her flesh, tasting her, devouring her. Delaney moaned and moved closer, straddling his legs. Fingers threaded in his hair, she pulled back his head and lowered her mouth to his.

Her hair fell over him like a red curtain, sparking awareness. He'd wanted this, wanted her, for a very long time. It seemed like ages.

She lowered onto him, the blanket falling away completely. That scrap of silk pooled at her waist and barely reached the tops of her thighs. With her legs surrounding him, he could feel the tantalizing heat of her. Moving his hands to the generous curve of her hips, he slid her along the throbbing length of him. They groaned in unison, agreeing for the first time.

He should stop this, he knew. But raw, primal need drove him now.

The kiss turned fierce. Wild. On her own, she rocked her hips in a rhythm that threatened to unman him. It felt impossibly good. Somehow, he knew this *all-or-nothing* woman would be the end of him.

Griffin needed to stop. This was madness. He was too close to the edge. Too close to losing control. He stilled her hips, earning a groan of frustration from her. "Delaney, I—"

"Please," she whispered, imploring him with those deep violet irises. The taste of her sweet breath filled his mouth. She strained against his hold.

He nearly embarrassed himself by coming apart in his breeches. His own release was close. Too close. But he couldn't deny her. Slowly, he brought his hand to the core of her desire. Fingers brushing against the soft curls, they were instantly damp. A choked sound of pleasure tore from his throat. What he wouldn't give to be inside her.

She held his gaze, her eyes hooded with passion. He followed the seam of wet heat, stroking her flesh. A sound, almost a whimper, came from her open mouth. He wanted to memorize every part of her, every nuance of texture and heat. She was silk and velvet, slick and white-hot. He delved into those wondrous swollen folds to the ripe bud awaiting his touch. "So perfect," he breathed.

And with the barest touch, she shuddered. Neck arched, her hips jerking in unmistakable release. "*Griffin!*"

Delaney collapsed against him, her breath heaving in and out of her lungs. Her inner flame was alive and brighter than ever.

There was no denying it any longer. She was in love. She'd known it for weeks. Maybe even longer. She loved Griffin Croft. And it frightened her to death.

Yet at the same time, it felt impossibly good. Especially when he'd said she was perfect and just as he'd imagined. He'd fantasized about her—*her!*

He was breathing hard, too, his head hanging over the back of the chair, his arms slack by his sides. He turned his head and drew in a breath. "Mmm…I never should have underestimated the passion of a woman whose hair smells sweet, like rain and fire combined. I must be on my guard in the future, so that I am a fit husband. I very nearly embarrassed myself."

Delaney shot away from him in a flash. With her legs still trembling, she stumbled slightly. "Husband?" She struggled to pull up her chemise and slip her arms through the straps. "We are not getting married."

The look he gave was one of bewilderment. "After what has transpired? Oh yes, we are. I am not a man who would sully a young woman's reputation and not make amends."

"I have not been sullied. Only…pleasured," she admitted, solely out of requirement. Suddenly, she felt foolish and embarrassed. "No barrier has been breached."

"Believe me, had it not been for the buttoned fall of my breeches your *barrier* would no longer exist." Frowning, he stood. "Your passion rivals my own. In fact, you nearly unmanned me. There is only one acceptable conclusion for two such like creatures."

She swallowed, unable to fight the urge to look down. There, she noticed an unmistakably thick bulge that moved as she continued her intimate examination. Had she really been close to unmanning him?

"If you would like, I could prove it to you," he said, as if she'd spoken the question aloud. He took a step toward her. "In addition to removing you of your barrier and any further doubt of how well matched we are."

Her gaze snapped up to his. "That won't be necessary."

"I wasn't speaking of necessity," he said, low enough that she barely heard him, his gaze making an equally intimate perusal of her body. "Then again, perhaps *necessity* is the correct word after all."

A confusing mixture of sensations moved through her. A pleasant, pulsing heat throbbed between her thighs, urging her to step forward and return to his embrace. On the other hand, her lungs seized and burned, compelling her to run from him. He expected to marry her?

"You've nothing to fear from me," Griffin said quietly. The passion that was in his gaze a moment ago seemed suddenly doused by concern.

"I'm not afraid of you." Stepping around him, she reached for her slightly damp petticoat and slipped it over her head. "I just don't want to marry you."

"You'll have to get used to the idea." He crossed his rather impressive arms over his chest. There was no amusement or teasing in his expression.

She glared at him. Did he actually believe she would simply give in to his demands? *Arrogant, conceited man!* "In case you have forgotten, we require different things. You require a wife who will give you an heir. I require a marriage in name only; ergo, no children and no true husband, *fit* or otherwise."

He smirked at her. "After what you've shown me this afternoon, I know very well that you require a husband in the truest sense—and often."

"You will have to be that husband for someone else," she said, gritting her teeth. She tugged her dress free of the branches as well. Slipping it on, she tied the inner tapes before fastening the bib front to conceal her breasts.

Throughout the entirety of her dressing, Griffin didn't say a word. He merely watched, as if every movement she made was meant for his pleasure. "I'm afraid my mind is made up. You're the only woman I want to marry. Though…I do not want a long betrothal. I believe I will speak to your father in the morning."

She yanked too hard on her stocking, and it ripped apart on the branch. All the breath left her lungs in a sudden whoosh of dread. "You cannot!" Even though she yelled it, the words came out a mere whisper. Tears suddenly filled her eyes. "Griffin, please don't do this. I cannot marry you." She absolutely refused to repeat her mother's mistake.

He came forward and took her in his arms, smoothing the hair back from her face. "Don't be afraid. I cannot bear it."

Did he think she was afraid of him? Guilt filled her at his incorrect assumption. She shook her head and reached up to brush her hand against his cheek. "I'm not afraid of *you*. Believe me, if I were a different person, I would be the happiest woman in the world to accept your offer." She lowered her hand. "But the woman I am *cannot* marry you."

His nostrils flared as he released her and crossed the room. He jerked open the door and stood still for a long while, staring out at the copse of trees and beyond, as if to find a solution. But she knew there was none. The simple truth was, she could not marry him, because she loved him far too much.

She folded the remains of her stockings in her hand and stepped into her soggy, ruined slippers. Before she could walk to the door, he turned.

"Then we will marry in name only."

Delaney rarely cried and she never expected to do so in front of Griffin. The fountain she'd suddenly become annoyed her. Hot tears burned as they forged a path down her cheeks, dripping onto the damp muslin. "I am sorry, Griffin, but I refuse to do that to you."

"This makes no sense at all. If you would just tell me—"

"Please," she said, lifting her hand to his mouth to silence him. "If you care at all for…my honor, please let me return to the house, and don't follow too closely behind."

He withdrew a damp handkerchief from his waistcoat pocket and dried her tears before pressing the soft linen into her hand. "I won't follow too closely, but I will come to call on you tomorrow."

She nodded and walked out of the little cottage without looking back. As for tomorrow, she planned to be far away from Danbury Lane.

CHAPTER SIXTEEN

Delaney McFarland had refused him. Griffin had offered her everything she wanted and yet, she'd still refused him. For the life of him, he couldn't understand her reasoning.

At his aunt's house, he hadn't had the chance to speak with her. They'd returned separately, but soon after he'd walked through the door, his mother had whisked his sisters, along with Delaney and her sister, into the waiting carriages without so much as a word to him. He'd been left to wonder what he could have done to earn such a rejection, first from Delaney and then from his own mother. In the end, he'd spent the entire ride back into town in trying to figure it all out.

Hours later, he still didn't have a clue. Did Delaney's desire to have a marriage in name only truly have everything to do with money and her desire to have control of her own fortune?

But hadn't his involvement with the young men of Warthall Place reassured her on *that* account?

"Griffin, come in here."

He'd been wandering the halls of the house after everyone else had gone to bed, or so he thought. Only now did he realize he stood directly outside his father's study. The last time he'd looked at his surroundings, he'd been in the upstairs gallery.

He moved into the room. "Yes, sir?"

His father's face was lit by a brace of candles beside him. And for some reason, he didn't look pleased. "Sit down. I want to speak with you in regard to your behavior this day."

George Croft wasn't usually so abrupt. Concern filled Griffin as he sat on the edge of the chair across from his father. Had something happened earlier that he didn't know about?

Looking at his father now, he wondered how he could have thought that the man no longer possessed command of that large wingback chair. If so, he was merely fooling himself. Right now, Griffin felt as if he were ten years old. "My behavior?"

"Your mother informs me that Miss McFarland was alone in that little cottage in Springwood during a storm," George Croft said, his voice hard and disapproving. "In that same span of time, you rode off to look for her. Yet according to both you and Miss McFarland, *you* never made it to the cottage."

Griffin sat up straighter. "Yes, sir." At least that was the story they'd agreed upon. He claimed to have lost his seat and spent the entire time looking for his spooked horse.

"Had you been at the cottage earlier that day, perhaps?"

"No, sir."

His father released a long, drawn-out exhale. "Is there something that would explain how your mother spotted one of your monogrammed handkerchiefs in Miss McFarland's grasp when she returned to the house?"

He closed his eyes. *The handkerchief.* He'd been hoping to spare himself the humiliation of explaining what had transpired—how she'd refused him, not once but twice. He'd planned to leave tomorrow morning, speak with her father, and then come back shortly, announcing his engagement.

It was no use. "Yes. I found her in the cottage during the storm. Needless to say, we both knew what it would mean if we were to return to the house together after a lengthy time away." Griffin stood. Unable to contain his restlessness, he moved to the hearth. "Even so, I asked her to marry me."

His father looked at him with surprise. Then he smiled and laughed a familiar and hearty "Oh ho!" that had been heard more often when his father's heart was not as fragile.

"When your mother came to me with her suspicions, I must admit to being worried. After all, you've done nothing but pace the halls since," he said and made a sweeping gesture to him as Griffin poked the logs in the grate. "You can imagine my relief, though you are a sly devil, never to speak of your intent—"

"She declined, Father," he interrupted, still feeling the sting of it.

The iron poker clanged against the rack as he returned it to its place. "What's this? You finally find a woman you *want* to marry…" His father's expression altered once again, from happiness to speculation. "Or is there another reason you *must* marry?"

Griffin knew what his father was asking. "She is yet untried." Though not by any lack of desire on his behalf… or hers.

"Then you offered your hand in order to save her reputation."

"Yes." Griffin's hands flew up in an impatient gesture as he began to pace the room. "However, as I just mentioned, she declined the offer. That was when she asked to return to the house and for me not to follow too closely."

"Does she have designs on another gentleman?"

He believed matters were settled between her and Montwood. There were no other paupers in her sights that he knew of. "Not to my knowledge."

"And yet, by all rights and purposes, a Season in London indicates that Miss McFarland is open to the idea of marriage."

"Yes, sir. Just not to me, apparently." He stopped and gripped the back of the chair as if the action would keep him immobile inside. It didn't. So, he went back to pacing. "She wants a marriage in name only. Since I require an heir, she declined. And yet, even when I cast my own desires for my future—not to mention the security of my sisters—and offered to marry her in name only, she still declined, if you can believe it!"

The room fell silent. The events and disappointments of the day pressed on him.

"Then this is no passing flirtation," his father mused calmly, which frustrated Griffin to no end. It was as if he hadn't been paying attention to the crux of the matter. "When a man is willing to set aside his own needs for that of a woman, there must be love involved."

"Of course there is. I love her! Otherwise, I'd never—" It took time for his own words to reach him after he cast them to the ceiling. But when they came back, he heard the truth for the first time. *"Blast it all,"* he whispered, mimicking a certain auburn-haired termagant.

He was in love.

"And did you tell her?"

"No, Father," he said absently, still reeling. He loved her. He loved Delaney McFarland down to the very fire that fed her soul. Why had it taken him so long to realize it? Surely if she knew how he felt, she wouldn't refuse him again. He knew she cared about him. He'd seen it in her eyes. She'd never looked at Montwood with such affection. If she had…

Then, I would have to kill Montwood, he thought with a laugh.

"Well, why not?"

"Because apparently, your son is a complete idiot."

Delaney had never run from any challenge in her life. Yet for the first time, she was doing exactly that. She'd spent the entire journey home from Springwood House fabricating a terrible but wholly necessary lie.

"In short, Emma needs me, and I will not abandon her," Delaney concluded. She managed to continue eye contact throughout the entire *untrue* tale.

After scrutinizing her for no fewer than four entire minutes without a word, her father offered a nod. Apparently, he was in no mood to argue.

Delaney did not pry. Instead, she turned to go to her room to pack a few things. She was grateful that convincing him had been so simple. One must not look a gift horse—

"Before you go," he said, his commanding tone raising the downy hairs on her nape.

She stilled and then slowly turned back. "Yes, Father?"

Gil McFarland's thick wiry brows straightened into a flat line over his icy blue gaze. "Miss Pursglove is not my only source of information regarding your behavior. I trust you understand what is expected of you."

Under normal circumstances, such a statement would raise her ire. She loathed being treated like a wayward youth instead of a fully grown woman of marriageable age.

Marriageable... Griffin Croft had proposed marriage. She still couldn't believe it. More than that, she couldn't believe how much she'd wanted to accept. Yet when she'd refused him, he'd surprised her even more by offering her everything she wanted—a marriage in name only, the key to her freedom, a life without the fear of falling in love and having her heart torn to pieces.

The only problem was, she'd already fallen in love with him. Now her heart lay in a tangle like last Season's ribbons.

She could barely meet her father's gaze. "In regard to your expectations, I am without a doubt of my worth."

And with that, she quit the room while trying to hide the anguish she felt.

A short while later, Delaney stood in her chamber, packing only the essentials into a satchel.

Miss Pursglove entered her room without knocking, announcing her presence with an austere sniff. "Friend or not, if you leave before dawn as you've planned, irreparable damage to your reputation will result."

Delaney was in no mood for this. "I'm certain, with your extensive training, you've learned that eavesdropping is impolite."

"You are on the verge of breaching a line that can never be uncrossed," the wretched woman hissed. "Your behavior is unacceptable."

"Never fear, I'm sure Father will merely add to my dowry, making me irresistible," she spat back, hands on hips. Her temper was climbing quickly, as if in defense of her own broken heart. The rage felt much better than complete and utter despair.

Miss Pursglove sneered, her dark eyes narrowing as she stepped further into the room. "You are rich, to be sure, but there is a certain degree of character even the most basic husband requires."

"You forget yourself, Miss Pursglove," Delaney warned. "You are an employee, not a part of this family."

"Do not think for a moment that it has been easy for me to withstand the association. My only accomplishment here has been instructing your sister. You defy me *and* the rules of society, again and again. In the end, I cannot stand by quietly and let you sully my name as well." Raising her voice, she pressed a fist to the center of her own bosom. "If your father will say nothing, then it falls upon me. You will not leave this house!"

Delaney stared at her *decorum instructor*, with a mixture of fury and satisfaction seething within her. After all this time, she'd actually done it. She'd broken Miss Pursglove.

Striding across the room, Delaney retrieved a box from the bureau. "First of all," she began, her voice calmer than she felt, "you cannot tell me what to do. Frankly, I'm surprised you even try." She moved toward Miss Pursglove, a practiced smile on her lips. "Second, you cannot take any credit for my sister, because she has absorbed none of your overweening, condescending mannerisms. Even our father would agree, you were never hired to instruct her. Therefore," she said, presenting the box containing the ugliest brooch in existence, "without my presence in this house, you no longer have a purpose here."

Miss Pursglove blinked as her hand closed over the box.

"Consider that a parting gift," Delaney added, herding the apparently dumbfounded decorum instructor out of her bedchamber. "I could think of no other person who could make such an object look pretty by comparison."

And with that, Delaney closed the door as one would a pocket watch, with a satisfying click.

At an hour before dawn, she set off for Hawthorne Manor, Emma and Oliver's estate. First light had yet to bloom over the horizon. While she hated to arrive unannounced—and at such an unseemly hour—there was no help for it.

She had to leave London before Griffin Croft came to call and asked her to risk everything for him. Because for the first time, she was afraid she would.

Chapter Seventeen

"If you'll forgive me, sir, but the elder Miss McFarland is not at home."

Griffin didn't believe it for an instant. Most likely, she'd left instructions with her butler to state that she wasn't at home when he came to call. After all, he'd warned her in advance.

Thinking of her sitting up in her bedchamber with the belief that this would stop him, he almost laughed. "Then I should like to speak with her father."

"Mr. McFarland is not at home." The butler's expression gave nothing away.

Griffin bit back an oath and took a deep breath. "Would you be able to tell me when he might return?"

"I'm not at liberty to divulge Mr. McFarland's schedule, sir."

This was obviously getting him nowhere. "Would the younger Miss McFarland be receiving callers, then?" If the butler uttered another excuse, so help him, Griffin was going to explode.

"If you'll forgive me, sir—"

"Mr. Croft! What a coincidence," Bree McFarland said as she descended the stairs behind the butler. "I was just heading out now to see your sisters. Am I mistaken, or did I hear you ask Hershwell if I was at home?"

"Apparently, neither your sister nor your father is at home," he said, studying her closely for any sign of deception.

"Hershwell would lose his post if he revealed anything of father's whereabouts. As for my sister, I'm surprised you've not heard. It was such a big fuss. Last night when we arrived home, Delaney told Father that she'd received a message from one of her friends requesting her assistance on an urgent matter. Though I do not know the particulars, I do know that she had to leave before dawn this morning."

"On an urgent matter," he parroted, keeping the disbelief from his voice. He suspected the *urgency* had everything to do with his promising to call on her this morning. That was fine with him. He could wait her out. "Then I'll return later this afternoon."

He bowed and turned to leave.

"Mr. Croft," Bree McFarland said, stepping out to follow him. "I don't believe she'll have returned by then. You see, her maid informs me that she packed a bag to take with her, because she was removing herself from town."

He hesitated, a feeling of dread funneling through him like water being pulled on a drain. "And you've no idea where she's gone?"

"Delaney wouldn't have told me." She looked sideways as if embarrassed. "I haven't exactly been known for my ability to keep a secret for long."

Her admission brought out a new concern. If he was trying to win Delaney's favor, then it wouldn't suit his purpose to have rumors of his intentions all over town before he'd secured her. "Perhaps it would be best if we kept this exchange between us for the time being."

And he would have to be careful how he sought information on her whereabouts in the future.

When Griffin spotted young Mr. Simms before he left Danbury Lane, he learned that the lad knew nothing of Delaney's departure either, other than the fact that she'd left shortly before dawn. Not only that, but she'd taken one of her father's carriages and drivers with her. Neither the driver nor the carriage had returned, which left Griffin with only one conclusion. Somehow, he'd lost her.

Of course, he wasn't one to accept defeat. He would simply find her by any means necessary.

Frustrated, Griffin went to Gentleman Jackson's saloon. He needed to find a decent sparring partner. As luck would have it, Everhart was there.

Today, however, his opponent was sorely lacking in skill. Griffin's fist connected with flesh time and again. "You're an easy target today, Everhart. Spend the night carousing?"

"Though you may not believe it, I kept very respectable company last evening," he said through a yawn and then threw a punch that struck only air. "My cousin and his wife invited me to dine with them. Afterward, Rathburn gave me leave to stay in my usual guest quarters if I chose, and so I did." This time, he blocked the blow to his gut. "Regardless,

I was not expecting to awaken at dawn to the sound of some red-haired demon pounding on the door."

Griffin's arms felt suddenly stiff and leaden. "Red-haired demon?"

Everhart took advantage with a left and then a right to his ribs. "With my room overlooking the drive and receiving the full force of those violent raps, I stumbled out of bed and stuck my head out the window." Dancing from foot to foot, he motioned with his fist for Griffin to raise his guard again. "Anyway, I learned later that the chit was one of my new cousin-in-law's friends, requesting use of Rathburn's hunting box in Scotland. Apparently, she had to flee posthaste, though my cousin and his bride could only speculate over the reason. If you can believe it," he paused to laugh with incredulity, "Emma said that only a matter of the heart could be the cause. Besotted fool that my cousin is, Rathburn was inclined to agree."

Griffin stilled. *A matter of the heart.* That was reason she'd left London. Could it be that Delaney McFarland was in love with him?

Everhart connected with Griffin's jaw and knocked him flat.

Blinking the stars from his eyes, Griffin looked up. "Whereabouts in Scotland?"

"Near Dumfries. I've stayed there a time or two. Say, are you going to sit on the floor, or are we going to finish?" Everhart offered his assistance.

Dumfries? Surely, fate had a hand in this. Griffin stood and shook his opponent's hand. "I owe you one, my friend."

"For knocking you on your arse?"

"Precisely."

CHAPTER EIGHTEEN

Outside Dumfries, Scotland

Groggy, Delaney sat up in bed and pushed a mass of red tangles from her face. She stretched, only to discover that nearly every muscle in her body ached. How was it possible to sit in the back of a carriage for the better part of six days—not counting stops for meals, a change of horses, and a night's rest—and still be exhausted after arriving at her destination?

Yesterday afternoon, when Rathburn's housekeeper had opened the door of the spacious stone and shingle hunting cottage, the first thing out of Delaney's mouth had been a yawn.

Mrs. Shaw had immediately escorted her to a guest room, where Delaney had summarily fallen asleep. And by the look of the sun rising over rolling hills in the east, she'd slept all through the night, as well.

Looking down, she noted that she still wore her traveling costume. Her very wrinkled traveling costume. She'd just begun to unbutton the dark blue jacket when she heard whispers in the hall outside her door.

"Arriving with nae maid *and* in such a rush, I dinna ken what to think," Mrs. Shaw said in her thick Scottish burr. "Be that as it may, His Lordship's missive left explicit instructions to treat her lik' family, for she is one of the new Viscountess's closest friends."

Delaney smiled at that, glad to have such good friends to support her, even when she hadn't given them a reason. She'd been afraid that if she'd spoken the reason aloud, she would have crumpled to the floor in a heap of sobs.

Now, a safe distance away from the cause, she stood up and walked to the window to open the sash. The cool breeze was sweetly scented by the dewy grass, moss, and heather. Down a gently sloping hill stood the abbey ruins and beyond those, a tree-lined stream curled toward a grand estate, miles in the distance. The lovely view gave her a sense of peace she hadn't felt for the past week.

At least, she had the comfort of knowing she was right to refuse Griffin. Because in the end, it was too easy to imagine her life in parallel to her parents. She couldn't bear to live like a haunted mirror image of her mother's broken heart. If Delaney married Griffin for the sake of his misguided honor, and he never loved her in return, the damage would be irreparable.

Looking into this future was bleak indeed. She would find herself spending years, always remembering how much she loved him. Ultimately, marrying for love was not an option for her. She refused to sentence herself to the life of her parents. By rejecting Griffin's suit, she'd made sure of it.

Delaney drew in a breath. Unfortunately, there was no answering heat. No assurance that her inner flame existed. It had completely sputtered out beneath the torrent of sobs she'd released on her journey along the Great North Road.

She supposed she would have to learn to live without that part of her. Just as she would live without ever seeing Mr. Croft again.

She wouldn't return to her father's house, either. She was putting that life behind her as well. Instead, she planned to pen a letter to Mr. Harrison, inquiring if she could work for him at Warthall Place until a school for girls could be established, preferably far away from London. At least, that way she could achieve her dream of helping those children, and in return, she would fulfill her own sense of purpose, which was all she really needed.

A soft knock fell on the door a moment before it opened. Beneath a ruffled cap and a few graying strands at her temples, the older woman smiled. "Guid. Ye'r awake at last. I've brought a cuppa, Mrs. MacRyrie's bannocks, and some heather honey to git ye settled." She set the tray down on a bench at the foot of the bed and poured tea into a waiting cup. "And of course. ye'll be wantin' a bath. We're already heatin' the water. Nothin' finer than a bath efter a lang journey."

"Thank you, Mrs. Shaw," Delaney said, grateful but still not wanting to reveal too much.

The woman came near and offered the cup. "I'll launder yer clothes, since the satchel you brought is on the wee side. I'm sure you'll be wantin' somethin' fresh to wear."

Delaney curled her hands around the cup, welcoming its warmth as another cool breeze rushed in through the window. "I packed two more dresses, though they are far less substantial than what I'm wearing. I imagined it would be warmer since we've reached the end of June."

"*Ach*, but 'tis warm." As she spoke, she flitted about the room, straightening up the bed, tossing Delaney's discarded jacket over one arm. "I'm certain we hae a nice woolen shawl for ye, if ye get too cold."

"That's very kind of you. I'd like to walk a bit this morning." A very long walk would help to clear her head. Delaney took a sip and pointed out in the distance. "How many miles away would you say that estate is?"

From her vantage point, the house stood as tall as the trees surrounding it, though that did little to aid her in assessing its size. Yet something about the dark brick façade, trimmed with pale stone around each window and door, appealed to her.

"That'd be Brannaleigh Hall, the summer home of the late Viscount Brinley. It's been empty for nigh on three years, though the caretakers, Mr. and Mrs. Culloden, keep it in fine shape." She came up to peer out the window and used her apron to rub at a mark on the sill. "I must warn ye, it's a fair stretch of the legs."

"That's exactly what I'm after," Delaney said but felt little conviction. She needed to get a sense of herself back. "I'll explore the grounds after my bath."

"Guid," the housekeeper said with a touch of concern as she tapped her on the shoulder. "That'll get ye settled straightaway."

Settled into her new life.

But Delaney doubted that a bath could wash away the old one.

Dressed in a somber slate blue to match her mood, Delaney walked down the stairs. She'd attempted to tame her hair into a braid, but already her efforts were snaking wildly about her cheeks and throat as a breeze came in through the open front door.

"There ye are," Mrs. Shaw said, walking briskly from the back of the house. "Mrs. MacRyrie packed a special lunch."

Delaney took the small pail with the cheesecloth bundle inside. "Thank you. And please extend my appreciation to Mrs. MacRyrie as well."

The housekeeper smiled at that. "I'll have the kettle ready for yer return. And if ye need to speak about what troubles ye, I'll be glad to listen—" She stopped short at the sound of horse hooves galloping up the drive. "That'd be Douglas, Mrs. MacRyrie's son. He comes this way whenever his belly is empty, which is nearly every day—*Which* reminds me, I found this lovely maroon shawl in a chest belonging to the Dowager Viscountess Rathburn. Let me fetch it from the parlor before ye set off."

Delaney watched her disappear through the door leading off the foyer and caught sight of her own reflection in an oval mirror. Her simple day dress hosted a ruffled hem at the bottom and satin sash beneath her breasts but not a single flounce. Her small bosom was not disguised in any way—although, there was no one to notice it or to think she was perfect anyway. Ever again.

She sighed, wondering when she would stop thinking about Griffin Croft. *How long does it take to fall out of love with someone?*

Mrs. Shaw came out of the parlor and stopped beside Delaney, but her gaze was fixed on the door. "I guess it isn't Douglas, after all. I wonder who…"

The housekeeper's next words fell on deaf ears as Delaney turned and saw a figure emerge in the doorway. Her heart sputtered. The air left her lungs in a rush. "Mr. Croft!"

Beneath the archway, he bowed in greeting, his gaze never leaving hers. Somehow, he'd found her. And by the state of his windswept hair, poorly knotted cravat, and muddied boots, it hadn't been an easy journey.

She regretted every trial he'd gone through to get there.

But then he had to open his mouth and ruin everything.

"Good morning, *Mrs. Croft.*"

CHAPTER NINETEEN

"Ye'r married," Mrs. Shaw said, her Scottish burr rolling over the words so long they started to sound like church bells. Then, a wide grin filled her face, as if she suddenly understood a riddle.

Delaney shook her head. "We are not married."

"Perhaps not in the truest sense…" Griffin interrupted, a look of supreme triumph flashing in his gaze. "Yet."

If he thought that traveling all this way meant she would simply change her mind, he was sorely mistaken. Still…he said the words with such heated certainty that she had to blush.

"Ye poor wee lass." Mrs. Shaw sidled up to her and draped the heavy shawl around her shoulders. "Now I understand why ye looked so frightened and alone yesterday. Many a young woman has fled out of fear…and then regretted it later."

"Oh, but I didn't—" Delaney attempted a denial, but the housekeeper had a dreamy look in her eyes and wasn't listening anyway.

"That happened wi' Mr. Shaw and me, so many years ago. I was so young 'n' unsure that I ran away. He didn't find me for nigh on a month. Ah, but when he did, I was glad he was my husband already." She cast a knowing glance to Griffin, earning a chuckle that made Delaney's cheeks burn.

He lifted his shoulders in a helpless shrug, as if he hadn't any control over the older woman's incorrect assumptions.

"Though I cried for shame, because I'd wished that had been our wedding night." Mrs. Shaw nodded sagely and then took Delaney by the shoulders and turned her to face Griffin. "Now, what ye need to do is walk over to the smithy's 'n' say yer vows over the anvil. Ye can still have your weddin' night with nae regrets after."

Griffin smiled and proffered his arm. "And where is the nearest blacksmith?"

"Back toward town."

Ignoring his bent elbow, Delaney skirted around him. "Mr. Croft, might I speak with you in private for a moment."

"Certainly, *Mrs. Croft.*"

Delaney drew in a quick breath. In the same instant, she felt a familiar warmth ignite deep within her. Her inner flame had returned.

Griffin followed her out the door, fighting the urge to take her in his arms with every step and every angry swish of her braid. He wanted to kiss her until the crazed unrest that had claimed him this past week faded away. He wanted to slip that shawl from her shoulders, strip her bare, and make love to her right here, right now. He wanted to prove to her and to the world that she was his.

Suddenly, she turned on her heel, violet eyes blazing. "Stop this at once. I am not part of a cat-and-mouse game. You cannot chase me across the country as if you've the right. I am not yours."

Those last words came out as a taunt, testing the last of his control. "If you did not want me to chase you, then why did you run away? You could have remained in town and made your point perfectly clear by refusing my suit directly to your father."

"And risk his not listening to me, the same way you haven't?" She scoffed.

"It's not the same at all." He took a step closer and gently shook his head. "I listen to every word your lips speak. I hear every secret your eyes tell. I know exactly why you fled London. We both know."

Her perfect bosom rose and fell in rapid, shallow breaths. That haunted look he'd witnessed before flashed across her gaze. He regretted being the cause of it. Yet at the same time, he knew the cure.

"I realize now that my initial proposal did not convey the…the *depth* of my obligation to marry you," he said before taking a deep breath. Had he known how difficult it would be to tell a woman he loved her, he would have practiced on the way here. He felt his tongue thicken. His heart was beating so fast, he feared it would climb up his throat, fall out of his mouth, and drop onto the ground at her feet.

He was so concerned with his next words that he hadn't even noticed the alteration in her expression.

She took a step toward him and pushed the tip of her finger into the center of his waistcoat. "I believe we explored those shallow depths quite succinctly when I stated there was no *obligation* on your part."

He reached for her hand to press it flat over his chest, intending to for her to feel what he was trying to say, but she pulled away from him. Again.

"You've misunderstood," he said, frustration adding bite to his words. "I did not come here to continue this *cat-and-mouse* game, as you've called it. I came here to tell you—"

"Mr. Croft," the housekeeper called from the doorway. "Will you be needin' a room prepared?"

Delaney's gaze rounded, flitting from him to the door and back to him.

A sudden realization struck him. Here he stood, exhausted, covered in mud and filth from his journey, and steps away from an eager audience inside the house. Perhaps this was not the time to profess his undying love.

He dropped his head back toward the sky for an instant, exhaling deeply, and then he turned. "Thank you, no. I have a place nearby." And then to Delaney, he bowed. "It is probably best that I leave you now. I must warn you, however, that if you choose to flee before dawn on the morrow, I will find you again."

CHAPTER TWENTY

"I thought yer husband would hae returned yesterday," Mrs. Shaw said as she hung Delaney's clothes in the wardrobe the following morning. "Though perhaps he had a time findin' a room at the inn."

"I'm sure he managed quite well." Delaney refused to feel an ounce of guilt or attempt to explain that he wasn't her husband and that his remark had been said to incite her temper. Nothing more.

Nothing more? Even she had a difficult time believing there was nothing more between them. Griffin Croft wouldn't have come all this way merely to incite her temper. Then it stood to reason that *obligation* wasn't his sole purpose either. Yet that was precisely what he'd said.

"We get a terrible lot of travelers from London when it's near the end of spring, and the London Season starts to dwindle." The housekeeper draped a fresh petticoat and a lavender muslin dress, embroidered with yellow poppies at the hem, over the foot of the bed. "For some, love is a great race. They hae to get there as fast as they can. But they dinna ken how

patient it can be. True love stands back 'n' waits for the rush
to subside."

Delaney ignored the fluttering in her stomach. "Arrogant
men will do that too."

"Aye." Mrs. Shaw laughed. "But I doubt many arrogant
men will chase a woman across the country 'n' then let her hae
time to gather her bearin's."

"No," Delaney admitted quietly.

"Not unless…" the older woman mused, rocking back on
her heels.

"Unless, what?"

"He expects you to go to *him* this time." She gave an
absent shrug before she walked to the door. "Perhaps he only
wanted to make yer distance shorter, savin' ye the humiliation
of drivin' all the way back to London."

Delaney's mouth fell open on an argument, but the
woman had already closed the door. "He's not my husband,"
she hissed. Throwing the coverlet aside, she scrambled out
of bed.

Saving me the humiliation, she harrumphed. With a quick
jerk, she tossed her dressing gown to the bed and donned her
fresh clothes. She wished she'd brought sturdier stockings
because she planned to be out walking the entire day. That
way, if Griffin Croft had a notion that she was waiting here,
pining for him, he would quickly learn differently.

Now that her determination had returned, she wasn't
about to squander it by moping about as she had yesterday.
In fact, the only reason she pinned his handkerchief beneath
the bodice of her gown was to act as a barrier against the cool
breeze. Nothing more.

Within the hour, Delaney had a good leg under her.

Up ahead, she could hear water tripping over stones in the stream behind a bank of trees. Her stomach rumbled, and she was glad to have a luncheon packed by Mrs. Mac-Ryrie. She could even use the pail to collect buckle berries later on.

One thing was for certain, she would not spend another moment thinking about Griffin Croft. Or wondering if he'd found a room at the inn. A shiver brushed her as she thought of his being forced to ride into the next town to find shelter for the night. He had looked awfully exhausted.

"No," she told herself firmly as she lifted her skirts to cross over a fallen tree. "You will not think of Griffin Croft or worry for his welfare for another moment."

Just then, she heard a twig snap not too far from her. When she looked over her shoulder, her foot came down on a moss-covered stone and slid out from beneath her. Arms flailing, her body lurched. The pail flew from her fingertips. And then, all of a sudden, she found herself falling. Only not falling so much as being hauled against something. Or *some-one*, rather.

Griffin Croft held her soundly, his arms wrapped tightly around her waist. As if this happened all the time, her hands settled naturally atop his very broad shoulders.

Delaney blinked, disoriented. She'd been so distracted by her thoughts that she hadn't even noticed him. "Where did *you* come from?"

"Over the footbridge, and just in time too," he said with a smug grin. "Perhaps this rescue will earn me one more moment of your concern."

She pushed at his shoulders. "Mr. Croft—"

He kissed her quickly. "Hold that no doubt well-deserved set-down. There is something I forgot to tell you yesterday, and I was hoping you might help me remember."

It was difficult to pay attention to what he was saying when she couldn't stop staring at his mouth. It was such a lovely mouth too—perfectly formed, the flesh ridged with a series of infinitesimal vertical lines. She wondered, should he kiss her again more slowly, if she would be able to feel each one. "How could *I* possibly help you remember?"

No longer at risk of falling, Delaney realized she should probably demand that he release her. Even so, she found herself reluctant to leave his embrace, since this would be the last time. Falling in love with him had sealed her fate.

It only made sense for her to return to London as he'd suggested, refuse his suit directly to her father, and then never see him again. But was that what she truly wanted?

For now, she made a memory to take with her. She breathed in deeply. He smelled of clean linen and bay rum, his whiskers neatly shaven. His hair was thick and glossy from being damp. He didn't seem to mind when her fingers toyed with the shorter strands by his nape. And his cravat was in a lopsided knot, as if he'd dressed in a hurry.

"I'm so glad you asked." He brushed his lips across hers, slowly this time. A puff of warm breath followed, teasing the tip of her tongue and making it tingle. Even her breasts responded in kind. "I believe this is helping me remember a great deal."

Entirely flattened against him, her legs tangled with his, her belly in intimate contact with the thick, growing length of him, she easily confirmed that this was helping a *great deal*, *indeed*. Immensely so.

She followed his lips back and forth in a sort of mirrored pendulum. Then, he stilled so that her lips were the ones that brushed his. The soft friction shot spirals of heat through her body. And just like that, need ignited.

She pressed her mouth to his, running the tip of her tongue over his lips, tasting him. He growled in response. With hands splayed over her back, drifting lower to her hips, he pulled her tighter against him. Instinctively, she tilted her hips against him. But the action did not bring her the pleasure it had when she'd straddled him a week ago. Had it only been a week ago? Eons seemed to have begun and ended in this time apart.

Gripping her, he lifted her to her toes. This time, his hips tilted against hers. She groaned into his mouth. This was turning into more than a simple memory to take with her. A warning voice told her that if she continued, it would complicate matters immensely. And yet, try as she might, she couldn't stop.

Her tongue went on a frenzied exploration, tasting, flicking, suckling. She drank in the flavor and feel of him. Completely absorbed in the kiss, she paid no attention to how her hands stole around his neck to unknot his cravat. Not until she felt the warm flesh of his throat against her fingertips. But she couldn't stop there, not with his shirt gaping all the way down to the buttons of his waistcoat. There was much to explore. Much to commit to memory.

Griffin's hands seemed possessed by the same desire because in the next instant, she felt a tug as he untied one of the hidden fastenings of her dress. At the same time, her nimble fingers worked apart each waistcoat button and spread it apart, before she dragged his shirt free of his breeches, drawing out a hissed breath from him.

She pulled back to gaze down at what her hands had uncovered. He was glorious, all ridges and lines. A sculpture's dream. A woman's fantasy. This sight would be forever burned inside her mind.

One more tug and her dress fell open, sagging on her shoulders the same way his coat and waistcoat had on him. Then, they moved apart as one, shrugging off their outer garments before coming back together with burning open-mouthed kisses.

"How is your memory, Mr. Croft?" she asked as she lifted the hem of his shirt. With a quick movement, he jerked it over his head and tossed it to the ground. His flat nipples were much darker than her pale ones. Dusted with dark brown hair, his chest was firm as well and larger than hers. With anyone else, she would feel nervous and even ashamed by her lack of a bosom, but not with Griffin. He'd told her she was perfect. And now, she believed him.

Her petticoat was the next to go, up over her head.

"Improving by the moment."

Desperate to keep moving forward before her mind caught up with her actions and cautioned her against them, she stripped out of her chemise and leapt into his arms. He caught her on a groan. Lifting her so that her legs encircled his waist, his large hands cupped the very bottom of her…bottom.

"Am I too heavy for your lovely arms to hold?" she teased, giving the bulk of his muscles a squeeze.

"Not at all," he said with a grin and a swat on her bare flesh. "Nor are you too eager. We are equally matched in that ring. Somehow, I knew it would be like this."

"Oh, you knew, did you?" She smiled, feeling as if a sun glowed inside her. "Of all the men in the whole of England, I had to choose the most arrogant to love—" She froze, staring fixedly into his gaze.

The moment seemed to last forever. She held her breath. He held his. Had she said that aloud?

And then a slow smile spread over his face that might have seemed soft, if not for the conceited lift of his brows. "I knew that too."

He kissed her quickly, not allowing her time to recover from her sudden embarrassment or the irritation that nearly sparked. In fact, the longer he kissed her, the less she cared that he knew the depth of her feelings. She didn't want this to stop. She wanted this soon-to-be memory to linger on for days. She wanted to have her fill of him, if such a thing were possible.

The trees surrounding them concealed them from view. Directly overhead, the lacy canopy opened in a perfect circle, revealing a deep blue sky. The air smelled of clean shaving soap and the sweet scented water of the trickling stream beside them.

Atop the pile of his discarded clothes, Griffin lowered her to the ground. She could feel the buttons of his coat beneath her shoulders. Lying on her back, she watched as his gaze roamed over her face and drifted to her breasts. And when he licked his lips, it felt as if he'd drawn her flesh into his mouth. Her nipples puckered and tingled. She pressed her hands over them to stave off the burning ache that followed.

"Is that where you want me?" he asked as he moved to cover her, the short curled hairs of his chest brushing the backs of her hands.

She made a sound of acquiescence as he kissed her lips. Her body arched off the ground to rub against his. Lifting her fingers, she trailed her splayed hands from his chest to his shoulders and then over every inch of his torso. Between their bodies, her fingers flitted down to his breeches. The length of his manhood strained against the buckskin, compelling her exploration. He was so perfect and beautiful in every way so far that she was eager for the rest of him.

He tilted his head back on an oath, a muscle twitching in his jaw. "You test the limits of my control."

She smiled at that, pleased that she had this effect on him. "And you test the boundaries of my impulsivity. Apparently, I have none."

She wanted this. She wanted Griffin to make love to her. She'd wanted this for so long that she hardly imagined not always having felt this way.

Releasing the fall of his breeches, he bounded free, heavy and thick, into her waiting hand. Griffin groaned, his gaze molten and seething beneath the surface. That heat speared her, causing her blood to catch fire. She gripped him, shaping her hand around his considerable girth. When he closed his eyes and gritted his teeth, she was unsure if he liked it or not. However, when she slid her hand up to the tip and he groaned again, she had her answer. Repeating the action, she felt her own body respond, drawing up with that sensation of a reticule being cinched closed tightly. *Mmm…*

Griffin stilled her hand and withdrew from her grasp with a shudder. "Now for your torment, my fiery one."

Leaving her mouth, he brushed his lips along her jaw, down her throat, and to the hollow between her breasts. With his tongue, he outlined the teardrop shape of one breast and then the other. Her aching flesh throbbed. She wanted him to repeat what he'd done a week ago and to kiss her deeply. She'd never been good at waiting. Inside, she felt like a blaze burning out of control. Flames crackled beneath her skin.

Seeking something cool, she set her hands, palms flat, atop his coat. But it wasn't cool enough. His mouth moved inward now, tracing the same line but slightly closer to her aching center. Reaching out beyond his coat to the soft, cool grass beneath it, she sighed with a modicum of relief. Then his mouth closed over one agonized peak.

She combusted. Her arms rose to surround him, but he stopped her before she could complete the motion. With gentle pressure, he held them down. This forced her to focus on the feel of his tongue rasping against her flesh, the heat of his mouth as he drew her deeper. She released a choked sob. Arching her neck, her head rolled back as she gasped for breath. Just when she thought she couldn't take any more, he lifted away.

"I knew it would be like this," he growled against her lips, shifting between her thighs, urging her wider. Reaching down between them, he slid the length of his manhood against her, earning another gasp in response. "You're so hot here. Fire inside and out. That's what you are—a living, breathing fire."

Unable to form words, she nodded in agreement. He continued to slide his flesh against hers, over and over again. Now, with her arms free, she clutched him, rising up to press her mouth to his. In the same instant, he edged inside. Her body seemed to lock around him. She could feel every fine distinction of his shape, the heat of him, the ridge that teased the outer folds of her flesh.

"My firestorm," he said with a fierce kiss.

Then, he drove inside her. Fast. Hard. Ripping through her barrier. Stretching the swollen walls of her most intimate flesh.

She cried out. Her nails bit into his shoulders a moment before her hands fisted as she tried to push him away. "Griffin!" Hot, angry tears leaked from the corners of her eyes, trailing down to get caught in the whorls of her ears. "You're such a tyrant. You make me lie still for eons to endure your torment. You offer the sweetest pleasures. Whisper endearments from your lips. And then you impale me with that caber between your legs and make absolutely no apologies."

He chuckled against her mouth as he kissed her into silence. Cradling her face, he smoothed away her tears. "But I'm not sorry. There was no other way to get my *caber* inside of you." The arrogant man grinned down at her. "And if you would stop fuming for a moment, you'd realize your body isn't angry at me either. I can feel every one of your tremors. They grip me like a vise, inviting me deeper."

Only now was she aware of the subtle rocking motion of his hips. That swift searing pain had faded, merging into a different type of ache. He watched her closely. The raw intimacy in his gaze ignited a new fire within her. The flame consumed her and made her fully aware of the heated length of him buried inside her. Her body cinched around him tightly.

Griffin's eyes glazed over as he hissed a breath through clenched teeth. Moving within her, over her, he lifted her hips. Those tremors intensified. Did he feel it too?

He groaned in response.

Delaney kissed his jaw, the tight cording of this throat. They were connected so intimately, she wondered if he could feel the burning intensity of her love as well. Lifting her legs to surround his hips, she clung, matching his rhythm. Slick heat coated the length of him as he drove deep inside her. Waves of searing pleasure swelled within her, like a dam about to give way beneath a tide of molten heat.

"Yes," he whispered hotly against her lips, as if he felt it too. There was no stopping it. As his thrusts quickened, all thought fled. All she could do was hold on and—

Ah! The dam broke. Flames licked over her flesh, so hot they burned cool against her skin. She cried out again and again as the inferno consumed her. Griffin answered in kind. His shout echoed around them as he buried himself deep within her.

Together like this, they seemed more a part of nature than the grass and trees around them. No matter what happened now, her life would never be the same. And she would have a memory to keep with her always.

But would it be enough?

CHAPTER TWENTY-ONE

Griffin tugged on the familiar handkerchief pinned inside the bodice of Delaney's gown as he helped her dress. His knowing smirk earned him a swat of her fingers against his. This fearsome, fiery beauty loved him. And because he couldn't contain the joy he felt, he pulled her against him for another kiss.

She slanted her mouth across his, matching his hunger. Her lips parted to reveal the heat within her. He knew those internal flames quite well now. Already, he was eager to have her again, preferably in his bed. Not that the soft cushion of grass had been a deterrent in any way.

Of course, he hadn't intended to make love to her here. Then again, when had any of his plans turned out where Delaney was concerned?

This morning, from his window, he'd spied her walking toward the stream that separated them. As luck would have it, she'd been near the footbridge just as he was stepping across to join her.

Now, Delaney set her hands against his forearms before he could lower her to the ground once more. "I've been gone for hours. Mrs. Shaw might send someone looking for me."

He kept her close. "Then we won't let them find us. Besides, we have everything we need here. The convenience of a stream. The scattered remains of your lunch pail. We could forage, naked in the forest, for days…weeks, even."

"As much as I enjoy being naked with you, Mr. Croft," she said with a laugh against his lips. "I fear I would soon be forced to wear flower garlands and leaves. After all, I do enjoy clothes immensely."

"And yet you ran away from the shops of London." He brushed the hair from her face and gently tucked it behind her ear. "You ran away from me."

She shied away from his gaze. "It wasn't as easy as you make it sound."

"I was furious at first," he said without any of that anger in him. At the moment, he wouldn't know what anger was. He could only feel this pleasant, humming bliss. Taking her hands and gathering up her pail, he led them along the path toward the footbridge he'd crossed earlier. "I thought you were trying to prove a point by asserting your independence. Then I realized I was angry at myself for how horribly I'd botched my proposal. I thought the depth of my feelings were evident when I offered you exactly what you wanted—a marriage in name only. After all, I was willing to sacrifice every need of my own just to be tied to you, in separate houses or not, for all the days of my life." He looked at her as he said the words, his hands settling on her waist. Delaney's eyes were wide and pale, like amethyst jewels. Leaning closer, he kissed her parted lips. "Now, however, I know I cannot take any separation from you. I love you far too much."

At last, the words that had been trapped inside him for a week were out. He marveled at the sense of release and lifted her high in a spin as they came to rest on the other side of the bridge.

It took a moment for him to realize that Delaney wasn't sharing his joy.

He set her down slowly as cold suspicion trickled through him. "Surely after everything that's transpired, you knew the outcome."

Now, all the color drained from her cheeks. "Griffin, I still cannot marry you."

"You have proven enough times that you are capable of anything you set your mind to," he said, his jaw clenching until he feared it would crack. "I believe what you are intending to say is that you will not. You *choose* not to marry me. After all, the word *cannot* suggests you have no choice in the matter."

"But I don't have a choice," she pleaded, her gaze softening as she lifted her hand to his face. "You know my reasons."

He drew her hand away and took her by the wrist. "To hell with your reasons! Do you think I care a fig for your fortune?"

Pulling her alongside him, he started to walk in the direction of Brannaleigh Hall, not two miles from there. Cresting the low hill beside the bank and away from the trees, they reached the long drive. "Look there, up the path. Could your fortune buy such a grand house and keep it in good standing for your lifetime and the next?"

"I don't know," she said, out of breath but keeping pace with him. "Perhaps." She tugged on his arm in order for him to turn to her, but he stayed the course.

He had a point to make, once and for all. "What about two houses?"

"Not likely. You know very well that I'd want part of it to go to Warthall Place." The last of her words were said with a bit of ire.

Good. If he was angry, he wanted her to be as well. "Wouldn't you think that the man who possessed such a house had a fortune of his own?" Apparently, the woman who'd employed a spy to track his social calendar hadn't bothered to inquire about his wealth or lands. That same woman likely knew every detail concerning each destitute reprobate amongst the *ton*. The fact that she'd never once looked into *his* background only made her goal, from beginning, all the more plain.

"Griffin, I don't care about the man who owns this house. Can you please stop this and let me return?"

He did stop and turned sharply to face her. "Only a moment ago, you claimed to love the man who owns this house."

The instant he said the words, he released her. Delaney felt the loss of his touch as quickly as a bucket of water douses a single flame. "Mrs. Shaw said it belonged to the late Viscount Brinley."

"And he was the Earl of Marlbrook's son," he said succinctly before he began to walk up the drive again. "Without an heir, the courtesy title passed to my father, who bequeathed the estate to me."

She'd known Mr. Croft would eventually inherit an earl-dom and therefore wasn't a pauper, but she'd had no idea he had a considerable fortune of his own. *That* was why he didn't care a fig for hers. He'd never cared. A strange, terrifying thrill sprang to life inside her. *All he wanted was her.* The words kept turning around and around in her head as she followed him the rest of the way in complete silence.

Within half an hour, he stopped in front of the wide white door and spoke briefly with the manservant.

Once the servant disappeared, Griffin gestured to dark brick façade of the house. "Here is Brannaleigh Hall," he said with a measure of resignation before he stepped over the threshold.

Still reeling and stunned, she followed him inside. An expanse of white marble tiles veined with grays and silver covered the foyer floor. The furniture and the chandelier over-head were draped in white sheets. The walls were painted and trimmed in white as well. She was very glad that she wasn't holding a glass of red wine, for she'd be the first to spill it.

Griffin swept his arm into the space around him. "Here is the hall where I first arrived yesterday, exhausted and weary, but also exhilarated because I'd just come from seeing your face."

She drew in a quick breath. There was no mockery in his tone but only more resignation. Lifting her gaze to search his face, she caught only his profile before he turned and began up the stairs.

At the very top, he walked down a wide hall trimmed in white wainscoting. *More white?* Imagine the disaster she would bring to such a pristine hallway. The lack of color was starting to tweak at her frayed nerves.

At the end of the hall, he turned and walked through an open door. It wasn't until she followed that she realized it was an expansive bedchamber, accented in pale gray silks, from the walls to the coverlet.

Griffin didn't look at her but stared at the bed, his expression hard and inscrutable. "Here is the bed where I spent hours dreaming of you last night."

Of *her*, not her fortune.

And then he walked past her and out into the hall again. The other doorways were closed and likely had sheets covering all the furniture. At the end of a second hall was a wide window facing west, with the light from the setting sun filtering in. The room beside it opened up to a grand portrait gallery.

"Here is the hall of my ancestors. You might recognize the one on the end as my father's portrait. One day, mine will hang beside his." Now, he faced her. The blue and brown of his irises shifted in the light as his gaze dipped from her face down to her stomach. "And my son's will hang beside mine."

His son. Automatically, her hand splayed over her abdomen, as if to protect the mere idea of his child. "It is unlikely that"—she swallowed down a sudden rush of sadness—"this afternoon will result in a child. The women in my family do not conceive easily." It had taken her mother two years and her aunt five. She could only assume the same would be true for her. Then again, she'd never allowed herself to imagine having a child until now.

Griffin stared at her, his face unreadable. After a moment, he shook his head and scrubbed a hand over his eyes. "Your words would make a sane man breathe a sigh of relief and run in the opposite direction. And yet, here I stand, contemplating ways to prove you wrong. To prove that you are not like any other woman, within your family or outside of it."

"Stop making me love you more," she pleaded, aching with need to leap into his arms. The distance between them felt like a tide, pulling her to him. She didn't know how much longer she could resist. She took a step back and then another. "Loving you has doomed me to a lifetime of misery."

He recoiled as if her words were the lash of Dorsey's whip. "Why would you say such a thing?"

"Because I cannot marry you, but I fear I will always love you and want to be with you."

"Then be with me!"

"I'm too afraid, Griffin!" There. Now it was out. He had to understand. "You told your sisters that I'm fearless, but that was a lie. I've lived with this fear inside me since the moment I met you."

Instead of the truth making him understand, he seemed only to grow distant and more incensed. "*That* is the real reason you want a marriage in name only. So that you never have to risk your heart."

"I don't want what happened to my parents to happen to us. We are already fighting! What happens in a few years, after I've given you an heir, and you stop loving me? Will that pain drive me away, compel me to abandon my children and live in another country? I would rather be alone and miserable than bring that pain to our children." Like the last threads of a dream upon waking, her mind conjured an image of a small, perfect face sleeping peacefully in her arms... Then, it disappeared too soon.

"I am fighting *for* something, not against. There is a difference." He took a step toward her, hands open as if to pull her into his arms. And then he stopped. "You cannot say that you love me, yet you don't trust me with your heart or mine." His hands fell to his sides.

"It isn't about trust. Of course I trust—"

"I have ordered the carriage," he said, cutting her off. "Go now, before I further strip myself of honor."

From the window, Griffin watched the carriage drive away. He stood there until it disappeared from view behind the old abbey ruins, and there his gaze remained, amongst the crumbled walls and barren landscape.

He felt just as desolate. He'd poured out his heart, felt that unspoken connection—only to learn that his love wasn't enough for her. She would trust a stranger with her fortune, but she wouldn't trust the man she claimed to love with her heart.

CHAPTER TWENTY-TWO

Delaney lay in bed, listening to the steady beat of her heart. The resilience of that organ surprised her. She hadn't thought something so mangled and broken would make it through the night. And yet…it was still there, beating.

"Only to mock me, no doubt," she whispered to the empty bedchamber. Each double beat of her heart seemed to whisper Griffin's name with longing. "To make me live for the next forty years, each day wishing I could take back everything I said."

All this time, she was afraid of Griffin's breaking her heart, but in the end, she'd done it to herself. Even when confronted with the fact that her fortune didn't matter, she'd still refused him—which meant that the only thing truly keeping them apart was her fear.

But she already loved him—she couldn't change that. She couldn't go back to a time before she loved him, even if she wanted to. Terrifying or not, her heart, her mind, her entire being wanted Griffin Croft.

Was she willing to risk everything for him?

Yes! And gladly too. It was as if the answer had always been inside her, without question.

However, before her heart could mend and rejoice, she thought back to yesterday. He'd been so closed off before she left him. She realized the instant he'd finally heard her. Those lake-water eyes had gone still, with no love or passion churning beneath the surface. Griffin was so proud and in control. And yet, she'd stripped him of his honor by refusing his proposal after they made love. She'd hurt him, the wound evident in his cold demeanor. Delaney didn't think he could ever forgive her.

Thinking about it now, she was ready to curl onto her side and give in to another bout of self-deprecating misery, but just then, she heard a carriage not far in the distance.

She sat up quickly. "Griffin!" Perhaps he wasn't through with her after all. Perhaps there was still a chance to tell him that she was ready to risk her heart.

Racing across the room to the wardrobe, she hastily dressed. Without even bothering to brush her hair or don a sash, she raced out the door and down the stairs. Sadly, it wasn't Griffin she saw waiting in the foyer.

"Father?" Her heart shattered all over again. Tears flowed freely from her eyes. "What are you doing here?"

"I might ask the same of you," he said, setting his silver-tipped cane and top hat on a bench by the door. When he looked up at her, his face hardened. "Why are you crying?"

Her face hardened as well. He was the last person she wanted to see. Everything was his fault, after all. "You've doomed Bree and me to a life without love. You only care about money, and that's why Mother left."

"That's what you might think, but I won't hear it," he said, raising his voice for the first time in so long that she was taken aback. "Don't you realize that I've done everything to prove that I didn't need her money? I've so much wealth in land and trade that it makes her fortune a mere pebble in a quarry."

Money. She hated that her life had revolved around it. "Then why did you heap so much on me, making me a laughingstock amongst the *ton*?"

"That was never my intention. I didn't know any other way! That is what fathers do. I wanted to show them all that I didn't care a whit for what they said about me or my reasons for marrying your mother. She, on the other hand, cared too much," he said on an exhale that seemed to extinguish his anger. "Not only that, but I wanted them to see you, not the tragedy. So, I gave them something to gossip about. And I wanted to give you the chance to find someone worthy of you."

She blinked. Was this conversation actually happening… and with her father? Gil McFarland sounded as if he cared. It sounded as if he'd been listening all these years.

Then his face turned ruddy again, as if in warning. "And if you think for a moment that I didn't know about your idiotic scheme to marry a pauper, then you've underestimated me *and* the depths of my temper. I'll have that blasted Montwood wetting his trousers in three seconds."

Oh yes. It really was her father. "You came all this way because you thought I ran away with Montwood?"

"Buckley keeps me apprised of all your associations."

Buckley! All this time, she thought she had his devoted loyalty. "Where is the devious little scamp?" Then again, perhaps looking out for her was his way of being the most loyal.

"He fell asleep in the carriage."

"You let him ride in the carriage with you?" She grinned. "Who knew my father's heart was full of syllabub?"

"Never mind all that," he blustered and made an impatient gesture for her to give him the daughterly embrace he expected. "If you didn't come here to run away with Montwood, then why are you here?"

"Because"—she took a breath—"I needed to figure out what I really wanted."

"And have you?"

After pecking him on the cheek, she nodded.

He shook his head. "A little more than a week away from London gave you the answer, yet over a year away hasn't helped your mother."

"I know what might help her." Delaney recalled something Mrs. Shaw had said. "Give her fortune back. If it means nothing to you, then you have to prove it."

"But if she has her own fortune to do with as she pleases"— he swallowed—"then I could lose her forever."

It seemed that the fear of one's heart being broken ran in the family. "Do you truly have her now?"

As the words left Delaney's lips, a sudden sense of urgency filled her. What had she done to prove herself to Griffin? To prove to him that she would go any distance for his love? She knew what she wanted. So why was she standing here when Griffin Croft might be leaving Scotland at this very moment?

Delaney couldn't risk letting him get away. "Father, I have to go."

"What do you mean?" He frowned, turning blustery again. "I just arrived."

"There isn't time to explain." Before her father could argue, she rushed through the open door. Mrs. Shaw had been right—Delaney needed to go to Griffin. He'd come all this way for her. Now, it was time for her to prove how much she loved him.

She only hoped she wasn't too late.

Hurrying down the hill as fast her feet would take her, Delaney stopped short when she saw a figure emerge. Her breath escaped in a rush. There he was—Griffin Croft—striding up the hill and stirring the fog at his feet.

The moment he saw her, he smiled, and she knew that he'd forgiven her. She knew that she never should have let her fears speak for her. Instead, she should have let her heart speak all along.

Not hesitating, she ran straight into his arms.

He held her tightly and smoothed the hair from her face. "I never should have told you to leave. I know you're frightened," he said with kisses over her brow, down her nose, and across her cheeks. "I should have reassured you, told you that you never need to fear for the safety of your heart."

"I know. I should have trusted you all along. The truth is, the only one I didn't trust was myself," she admitted. "I *have* been known to make rash decisions, after all. And yet, you were the only one I carefully plotted to steer clear of. If that wasn't an admission of love from the first moment, then I don't know what could be."

He captured her lips, branding her forever.

"Mr. Croft!" her father bellowed from the top of the hill. "You'd better have plans to marry my daughter, or you'll find yourself in a sorry state."

"We are already married," Delaney called over her shoulder. Then she turned back to Griffin and lifted her gaze. "Would you care for a walk to the nearest blacksmith, Mr. Croft?"

This time, she didn't mind his arrogant grin one bit.

"It would be my pleasure, Mrs. Croft."

ACKNOWLEDGEMENTS

Thank you to my editor, Chelsey Emmelhainz, for your uncanny ability to spot plot holes, for helping me keep track of the series details, and especially for the smiley faces in the margins. ☺

Thank you to the entire Avon Impulse team for your hard work. And a special thanks to Emily Homonoff for your organizational skills and cheerful e-mails.

Thank you to my family and friends for laughing with me, just when I need it most. And thank you to my readers for all your support.

Don't miss the other Wallflower Weddings!
Keep reading for excerpts from

DARING MISS DANVERS

and

WINNING MISS WAKEFIELD

Now available from Avon Impulse!

An Excerpt from

DARING MISS DANVERS

---

*Oliver Goswick, Viscount Rathburn, needs money, but
only marriage to a proper miss will release his inheritance.
There's just one solution: a mock courtship with a trusted
friend. Miss Emma Danvers knows nothing good can come
of Rathburn's scheme. Still, entranced by the inexplicable
hammering he causes in her heart, she agrees to play his
betrothed despite her heart's warning: it's all fun and
games…until someone falls in love!*

"Shall we shake hands to seal our bargain?"

Not wanting to appear as if she lacked confidence, Emma
thrust out her hand and straightened her shoulders.

Rathburn chuckled, the sound low enough and near
enough that she could feel it vibrating in her ears more than
she could hear it. His amused gaze teased her before it traveled down her neck, over the curve of her shoulder, and down

the length of her arm. He took her gloveless hand. His flesh was warm and callused in places that made it impossible to ignore the unapologetic maleness of him.

She should have known this couldn't be a simple handshake, not with him. He wasn't like anyone else. So why should this be any different?

He looked down at their joined hands, turning hers this way and that, seeing the contrast, no doubt. His was large and tanned, his nails clean but short, leaving the very tips of his fingers exposed. Hers was small and slender, her skin creamy, her nails delicately rounded as was proper. Yet when she looked at her hand covered by his, she felt anything but proper.

She tried to pull away, but he kept it and moved a step closer.

"I know a better way," he murmured and before she knew his intention, he tilted up her chin and bent his head.

His mouth brushed hers in a very brief kiss. So brief, in fact, she almost didn't get a sense that it had occurred at all. *Almost.*

However, she did get an impression of his lips. They were warm and softer than they appeared, but that was not to say they were soft. No, they were the perfect combination of softness while remaining firm. In addition, the flavor he left behind was intriguing. Not sweet like liquor or salty like toothpowder, but something in between, something... spicy. Pleasantly herbaceous, like a combination of pepper and rosemary with a mysterious flavor underneath that reminded her... *of the first sip of steaming chocolate on a chilly morning.* The flavor of it warmed her through. She licked her lips to be certain, but made the mistake of looking up at him.

He was staring at her lips, his brow furrowed.

The fireflies vanished from his eyes as his dark pupils expanded. The fingers that were curled beneath her chin spread out and stole around to the base of her neck. He lowered his head again, but this time he did not simply brush his lips over hers. Instead, he tasted her, flicking his tongue over the same path hers had taken.

A small, foreign sound purred in her throat. This wasn't supposed to be happening. Kissing Rathburn was wrong on so many levels. They weren't truly engaged. In fact, they were acquaintances only through her brother. They could barely stand each other. The door to the study was closed—*highly improper*. Her parents or one of the servants could walk in any minute. She should be pushing him away, not encouraging him by parting her lips and allowing his tongue entrance. She should not curl her hands over his shoulders or discover that there was no padding in his coat. And she most definitely should not be on the verge of leaning into him—

There was a knock at the door. They split apart with a sudden jump, but the sound had come from the hall. Someone was at the front of the house.

She looked at Rathburn, watching the buttons of his waistcoat move up and down as he caught his breath. When he looked away from the door and back to her, she could see the dampness of their kiss on his lips. *Her kiss.*

He grinned and waggled his brows as if they were two criminals who'd made a lucky escape. "Not quite as buttoned up as I thought." He licked his lips, ignoring her look of disapproval. "Mmm…jasmine tea. And sweet too. I would have thought you'd prefer a more sedate China black with lemon. Then again, I never would have thought such a proper miss would have such a lush, tempting mouth either."

She pressed her lips together to blot away the remains of their kiss. "Have you no shame? It's bad enough that it happened. Must you speak of it?"

He chuckled and stroked the pad of his thumb over his bottom lip as his gaze dipped, again, to her mouth. "You're right, of course. This will have to be our secret. After all, what would happen if my grandmother discovered that beneath a façade of modesty and decorum lived a warm-blooded temptress with the taste of sweet jasmine on her lips?"

An Excerpt from

WINNING MISS WAKEFIELD

*When her betrothed suddenly announces his plans to
marry another, Merribeth Wakefield knows only a
bold move will bring him back and restore her tattered
reputation: She must take a lesson in seduction from a
master of the art. But when the dark and brooding rake,
Lord Knightswold, takes her under his wing, her education
quickly goes from theory to hands-on knowledge, and her
heart is given a crash course in true desire!*

"Now, give back my handkerchief," Lord Knightswold said,
holding out his hand as he returned to her side. "You're the
sort to keep it as a memento. I cannot bear the thought of
my handkerchief being worshipped by a forlorn *miss* by
moonlight or tucked away with mawkish reverence beneath
a pillow."

The portrait he painted was so laughable that she smiled, heedless of exposing her flaw. "You flatter yourself. Here." She dropped it into his hand as she swept past him, prepared to leave. "I have no desire to touch it a moment longer. I will leave you to your pretense of sociability."

"'Tis no pretense. I have kept good company this evening." Either the brandy had gone to her head, impairing her hearing, or he actually sounded sincere.

She paused and rested her hands on the carved rosewood filigree edging the top of the sofa. "Much to my own folly. I never should have listened to Lady Eve Sterling. It was her lark that sent me here."

He feigned surprise. "Oh? How so?"

If it weren't for the brandy, she would have left by now. Merribeth rarely had patience for such games, and she knew his question was part of a game he must have concocted with Eve. However, his company had turned out to be exactly the diversion she'd needed, and she was willing to linger. "She claimed to have forgotten her reticule and sent me here to fetch it—no doubt wanting me to find you."

He looked at her as if confused.

"I've no mind to explain it to you. After all, you were abetting her plot, lying in wait, here on this very sofa." She brushed her fingers over the smooth fabric, thinking of him lying there in the dark. "Not that I blame you. Lady Eve is difficult to say no to. However, I will conceal the truth from her, and we can carry on as if her plan had come to fruition. It would hardly have served its purpose anyway."

He moved toward her, his broad shoulders outlined by the distant torch light filtering in through the window behind him. "Refresh my memory then. What was it I was supposed to do whilst in her employ?"

She blushed again. Was he going to make her say the words aloud? No gentleman would.

So, of course, *he* would. She decided to get it over with as quickly as possible. "She professed that a kiss from a rake could instill confidence and mend a broken heart."

He stopped, impeded by the sofa between them. His brow lifted in curiosity. "Have you a broken heart in need of mending?"

The deep murmur of his voice, the heated intensity in his gaze, and quite possibly the brandy all worked against her better sense and sent those tingles dancing in a pagan circle again.

Oh, yes, she thought as she looked up at him. *Yes, Lord Knightswold. Mend my broken heart.*

However, her mouth intervened. "I don't believe so." She gasped at the realization. "I should, you know. After five years, my heart should be in shreds. Shouldn't it?"

He turned before she could read his expression and then sat down on the sofa, affording her a view of the top of his head. "I know nothing of broken hearts or their mending."

"Pity," she said, distracted by the dark silken locks that accidentally brushed her fingers. "Neither do I."

However accidental the touch of his hair had been, now her fingers threaded through the fine strands with untamed curiosity and blatant disregard for propriety.

Lord Knightswold let his head fall back, permitting—perhaps even encouraging—her to continue. She did, without thought to right, wrong, who he was, or who she was supposed to be. Running both hands through his hair, massaging his scalp, she watched his eyes drift closed.

Then, Merribeth Wakefield did something she never intended to do.

She kissed a rake.

VIVIENNE LORRET loves romance novels, her pink laptop, her husband, and her two teenage sons (not necessarily in that order...but there are days). Transforming copious amounts of tea into words, she is the author of "Tempting Mr. Weatherstone" in Avon Impulse's Christmas anthology *Five Golden Rings* and the Wallflower Wedding Series. For more on her upcoming novels, visit her at www.vivlorret.net.

Visit www.AuthorTracker.com for exclusive information on your favorite HarperCollins authors.

Give in to your impulses . . .
Read on for a sneak peek at three brand-new
e-book original tales of romance
from Avon Books.
Available now wherever e-books are sold.

FULL EXPOSURE
Book One: Independence Falls
By Sara Jane Stone

PERSONAL TARGET
An Elite Ops Novel
By Kay Thomas

SINFUL REWARDS 1
A Billionaires and Bikers Novella
By Cynthia Sax

An Excerpt from

FULL EXPOSURE
Book One: Independence Falls
by Sara Jane Stone

The first book in a hot new series from contemporary romance writer Sara Jane Stone. When Georgia begins work as a nanny for her brother's best friend, she knows she can't have him, but his pull is too strong, and she feels sparks igniting.

Georgia Trulane walked into the kitchen wearing a purple bikini, hoping and praying for a reaction from the man she'd known practically forever. Seated at the kitchen table, Eric Moore, her brother's best friend, now her boss since she'd taken over the care of his adopted nephew until he found another live-in nanny, studied his laptop as if it held the keys to the world's greatest mysteries. Unless the answers were listed between items b and c on a spreadsheet about Oregon timber harvesting, the screen was not of earth-shattering importance. It certainly did not merit his full attention when she was wearing an itsy-bitsy string bikini.

"Nate is asleep," she said.

Look up. Please, look up.

Eric nodded, his gaze fixed to the screen. Why couldn't he look at her with that unwavering intensity? He'd snuck glances. There had been moments when she'd turned from preparing his nephew's lunch and caught him looking at her, really looking, as if he wanted to memorize the curve of her neck or the way her jeans fit. But he quickly turned away.

"Did you pick up everything he needs for his first day of school tomorrow? I don't want to send him unprepared."

His deep voice warmed her from the inside out. It was so familiar and welcoming, yet at the same time utterly sexy.

"I got all the items on the list," she said. "He is packed and ready to go."

"He needs another one of those stuffed frogs. He can't go without his favorite stuffed animal."

If she hadn't been standing in his kitchen practically naked, waiting for him to notice her, she would have found his concern for the three-year-old's first day of preschool sweet, maybe even heartwarming. But her body wasn't looking for sentiments reminiscent of sunshine and puppies, or the whisper of sweet nothings against her skin. She craved physical contact—his hands on her, exploring, each touch making her feel more alive.

And damn it, he still hadn't glanced up from his laptop.

"Nate will be home by nap time," she said. "He'll be there for only a few hours. You know that, right?"

"He'll want to take his frog," he said, his fingers moving across the keyboard. "He'll probably lose it. And he sleeps with that thing every night. He needs that frog."

She might be practically naked, but his emphasis on the word *need* thrust her headfirst into heartwarming territory. Eric worked day and night to provide Nate with the stability that had been missing from Eric's childhood thanks to his divorced parents' fickle dating habits. She admired his willingness to put a child who'd suffered a tragic loss first.

But tonight, for one night, she didn't want to think about all of his honorable qualities. She wanted to see if maybe, just maybe those stolen glances when he thought she wasn't looking meant that the man she'd laid awake thinking about while serving her country half a world away wanted her too.

"You're now the proud owner of two stuffed frogs," she said. "So if that's everything for tonight, I'm going for a swim."

Finally, *finally*, he looked up. She watched as his blue eyes widened and his jaw clenched. He was an imposing man, large and strong from years of climbing and felling trees. Not that he did the grunt work anymore. These days he wore tailored suits and spent more time in an office than with a chainsaw in hand. But even seated at his kitchen table poring over a computer, he looked like a wall of strong, solid muscle wound tight and ready for action. Having all of that energy focused on her? It sent a thrill down her body. Georgia clung to the feeling, savoring it.

An Excerpt from

PERSONAL TARGET
An Elite Ops Novel
by Kay Thomas

One minute Jennifer Grayson is housesitting
and the next she's abducted to a foreign brothel.
Jennifer is planning her escape when her first
"customer" arrives. Nick, the man who broke
her heart years ago, has come to her rescue.
Now, as they race for their lives, passion for
each other reignites and old secrets resurface.
Can Nick keep the woman he loves safe
against an enemy with a personal vendetta?

The woman at the vanity turned, and his breath caught in his throat. Nick had known it would be Jenny, and despite what he'd thought about downstairs when he'd seen her on the tablet screen, he hadn't prepared himself for seeing her like this. Seated at the table with candles all around, she was wearing a sheer robe over a grey thong and a bustier kind of thing—or that's what he thought the full-length bra was called.

He spotted the unicorn tat peeping out from the edge of whatever the lingerie piece was, and his brain quit processing details as all the blood in his head rushed south. He'd been primed to come in and tell Jenny exactly how they were getting out of the house and away from these people, and now . . . this. His mouth went dry at the sight of her. She looked like every fantasy he'd ever had about her rolled into one.

He continued to stare as recognition flared in her eyes.

"Oh my god," she murmured. "It's . . ."

She clapped her mouth closed, and her eyes widened. That struck him as odd. The relief on her face was obvious, but instead of looking at him, she took an audible breath and studied the walls of the room. When she finally did glance at him again, her eyes had changed.

"So you're who they've sent me for my first time?" Her voice sounded bored, not the tone he remembered. "What do you want me to do?"

What a question. He raised an eyebrow, but she shook her head. In warning?

Nothing here was as he'd anticipated. He continued staring at her, hoping the lust would quit fogging his brain long enough for him to figure out what was going on.

"I've been told to show you a good time." Her voice was cold, downright chilly. Without another word she stood and crossed the floor, slipping into his arms with her breasts pressing into his chest. "It's you." She murmured the words in the barest of whispers.

Nick's mind froze, but his body didn't. His hands automatically went to her waist as she kissed his neck, working her way up to his ear. This was not at all what he'd planned.

"I can't believe you're here." She breathed the words into his ear.

Me either, he thought, but kept the words to himself as he pulled her closer. His senses flooded with all that smooth skin pressing against him. His body tightened, and his right hand moved to cup her ass. Her cheek's bare skin was silky soft, just like he remembered. God, he'd missed her. She melted into him as his body switched into overdrive.

"What do you want?" She spoke louder. The arctic tone was back. He was confused and knew he was just too stupid with wanting her to figure out what the hell was going on. There was no way the woman could mistake the effect she was having.

She moved her lips closer to his ear and nipped his earlobe as she whispered, "Cameras are everywhere. I'm not sure about microphones."

And like that, cold reality slapped him in the face. He should have been expecting it, but he'd been so focused on getting her out and making sure she was all right. She might be glad to see him because he was there to save her, but throwing her body at him was an act.

Jesus. He had to get them both out of here without tipping his hand to the cameras and those watching what he was doing. He was crazy not to have considered it once he saw those tablets downstairs, but it had never occurred to him that he would have to play this encounter through as if he were really a client.

He slipped her arms from around his neck and moved to the table to pour himself some wine, willing his hands not to shake. "I want you," he said.

An Excerpt from

SINFUL REWARDS 1
A Billionaires and Bikers Novella
by Cynthia Sax

Belinda "Bee" Carter is a good girl; at least, that's
what she tells herself. And a good girl deserves
a nice guy—just like the gorgeous and moody
billionaire Nicolas Rainer. Or so she thinks,
until she takes a look through her telescope
and sees a naked, tattooed man on the balcony
across the courtyard. He has been watching
her, and that makes him all the more enticing.
But when a mysterious and anonymous text
message dares her to do something bad, she
must decide if she is really the good girl she has
always claimed to be, or if she's willing to risk
everything for her secret fantasy of being watched.

An Avon Red Novella

I'd told Cyndi I'd never use it, that it was an instrument purchased by perverts to spy on their neighbors. She'd laughed and called me a prude, not knowing that I was one of those perverts, that I secretly yearned to watch and be watched, to care and be cared for.

If I'm cautious, and I'm always cautious, she'll never realize I used her telescope this morning. I swing the tube toward the bench and adjust the knob, bringing the mysterious object into focus.

It's a phone. Nicolas's phone. I bounce on the balls of my feet. This is a sign, another declaration from fate that we belong together. I'll return Nicolas's much-needed device to him. As a thank you, he'll invite me to dinner. We'll talk. He'll realize how perfect I am for him, fall in love with me, marry me.

Cyndi will find a fiancé also—everyone loves her—and we'll have a double wedding, as sisters of the heart often do. It'll be the first wedding my family has had in generations.

Everyone will watch us as we walk down the aisle. I'll wear a strapless white Vera Wang mermaid gown with organza and lace details, crystal and pearl embroidery accents, the bodice fitted, and the skirt hemmed for my shorter height. My hair will be swept up. My shoes—

Voices murmur outside the condo's door, the sound piercing my delightful daydream. I swing the telescope upward, not wanting to be caught using it. The snippets of conversation drift away.

I don't relax. If the telescope isn't positioned in the same way as it was last night, Cyndi will realize I've been using it. She'll tease me about being a fellow pervert, sharing the story, embellished for dramatic effect, with her stern, serious dad—or, worse, with Angel, that snobby friend of hers.

I'll die. It'll be worse than being the butt of jokes in high school because that ridicule was about my clothes and this will center on the part of my soul I've always kept hidden. It'll also be the truth, and I won't be able to deny it. I am a pervert.

I have to return the telescope to its original position. This is the only acceptable solution. I tap the metal tube.

Last night, my man-crazy roommate was giggling over the new guy in three-eleven north. The previous occupant was a gray-haired, bowtie-wearing tax auditor, his luxurious accommodations supplied by Nicolas. The most exciting thing he ever did was drink his tea on the balcony.

According to Cyndi, the new occupant is a delicious piece of man candy—tattooed, buff, and head-to-toe lickable. He was completing armcurls outside, and she enthusiastically counted his reps, oohing and aahing over his bulging biceps, calling to me to take a look.

I resisted that temptation, focusing on making macaroni and cheese for the two of us, the recipe snagged from the diner my mom works in. After we scarfed down dinner, Cyndi licking her plate clean, she left for the club and hasn't returned.

Three-eleven north is the mirror condo to ours. I

straighten the telescope. That position looks about right, but then, the imitation UGGs I bought in my second year of college looked about right also. The first time I wore the boots in the rain, the sheepskin fell apart, leaving me barefoot in Economics 201.

Unwilling to risk Cyndi's friendship on "about right," I gaze through the eyepiece. The view consists of rippling golden planes, almost like . . .

Tanned skin pulled over defined abs.

I blink. It can't be. I take another look. A perfect pearl of perspiration clings to a puckered scar. The drop elongates more and more, stretching, snapping. It trickles downward, navigating the swells and valleys of a man's honed torso.

No. I straighten. This is wrong. I shouldn't watch our sexy neighbor as he stands on his balcony. If anyone catches me . . .